PREGNANT

BO...

BY
SUE MacKAY

Published in Great Britain 2017
By Mills & Boon, an imprint of HarperCollins*Publishers*
1 London Bridge Street, London, SE1 9GF

© 2017 Sue MacKay

ISBN: 978-0-263-92651-4

Our policy is to use papers that are natural, renewable and recyclable products and made from wood grown in sustainable forests. The logging and manufacturing processes conform to the legal environmental regulations of the country of origin.

Printed and bound in Spain
by CPI, Barcelona

Sue MacKay lives with her husband in New Zealand's beautiful Marlborough Sounds, with the water on her doorstep and the birds and the trees at her back door. It is the perfect setting to indulge her passions of entertaining friends by cooking them sumptuous meals, drinking fabulous wine, going for hill walks or kayaking around the bay—and, of course, writing stories.

Books by Sue MacKay

Mills & Boon Medical Romance

Reunited...in Paris!
A December to Remember
Breaking All Their Rules
Dr White's Baby Wish
The Army Doc's Baby Bombshell
Resisting Her Army Doc Rival

Visit the Author Profile page
at millsandboon.co.uk for more titles.

**Praise for
Sue MacKay**

'I highly recommend this story to all lovers of
romance: it is moving, emotional, a joy to read!'

—*Goodreads* on
A December to Remember

CHAPTER ONE

'THAT WAS TOO close for comfort.' Nurse Tamara Washington watched the paediatric intensive care team wheel their tiny patient towards the lift and PICC.

'Every parent's worst nightmare,' Conor agreed as he dropped onto a chair at the emergency department's work centre. 'At one point I didn't think we'd get him back.'

The baby had stopped breathing while being examined to find what was causing his dangerously high temperature.

'But you did. We did.' Sometimes it astonished her that they were able to revive someone so young and small. Always it shook her up. Today... Today it had been hard to hold her emotions in. Too close, too frightening. What-ifs played in her head as she stared at the man typing in notes on the baby's file. He needed to know.

'Have I grown a wart on the back of my head?' Conor asked in that Irish lilt that tightened her toes, and a whole lot of other areas of her body.

'Can you spare me a few minutes at the end of the day?' Tamara's chest clenched as her reluctant question came out. A few minutes that would change Dr Maguire's quiet, easy life for ever. No matter which path he took in response to the lightning bolt she had to deliver.

'Sure.' He tossed her a negligent eyebrows-raised

glance. 'What's bugging you? More stuff about med school?' He'd been more than patient with her over the application, and must think she was a pain in his gorgeous backside with her continual, often repetitive questions.

Tamara glanced around Auckland Central Hospital's ED, the place in which she felt most at home, and definitely most confident. This was where she knew her stuff.

'That's me. Crossing the "t"s and dotting the "i"s before I finally push "send".' Not even a reputed university had been going to get the better of her. These days she checked *everything*, over and over.

'Those "t"s and "i"s will be so crossed and dotted they'll be unrecognisable.' Conor gave her one of his dynamic, tummy-tingling smiles.

Except her stomach was far too tense to tingle. 'Today's the day I finish with it.' Literally. Trash-bin finish. Training to become a doctor was the dream she'd been working towards all year. The dream she was so invested in had turned to dust over a thin blue line on a plastic stick. Two test kits, different brands, same result. No argument.

Tamara's left hand pressed, oh, so gently on her unhappy tummy while her teeth worried her bottom lip. At least her mouth was better occupied doing that than spewing out any of the thoughts mashing her up on the inside. This being in charge of her life was full of pitfalls, all of them deep and dangerous. It was *her* life, right? Sometimes she wondered.

Conor cut through her worry. 'As long as the shift doesn't run over too much, let's go to the local for a drink and food.'

'No.' Nausea swamped Tamara at the thought of greasy pub food. As for alcohol, forget that for a while. Sweat saturated the folds of her baggy scrubs. Since the first tweak of nausea on waking last Friday morning she'd been in a terrible state, gutted at the abrupt about-turn in her well-laid-out, Tamara-controlled plans. Of course she'd fought the obvious, denied the deepening despair, knowing she'd lost another round in life's plans for her.

'Why not?' Conor looked bemused.

He hadn't spent the weekend fighting the inevitable. No, that started for him later today. 'Can we stick to your office?' So you can vent in private. 'I won't take up much of your time. Promise.'

His kingfisher-blue eyes widened briefly. 'This *is* about your application for university?' As head of this emergency department, Conor had backed her all the way when she'd decided to start studying extramurally with the goal of entering med school next year.

'For the absolute last time.' No doubt there.

'Right, my office when we're done with headaches and broken bones.'

His thick brogue wrapped around her, softening her heart when it needed to be steel, making her feel all mushy about him despite not wanting to feel anything for him. A sexy man with a whole lot more going for him, he was hard to ignore. They'd shared one night in his bed—with devastating consequences. No denying the tingle in her thighs and lower belly whenever he turned all Irish on her, though. But that was about the sex they'd shared. He'd been hot, and imaginative, and very, very good. Phew, her cheeks were warming at the memories. Of the sex. Nothing else. Sometimes she still pinched herself to make sure she hadn't imagined it. Now she had the evidence. No more pinches.

The strident sound of the buzzer from the ambulance bay curtailed any further discussion as Conor leapt up from the chair. 'Here's our guy.' A car-versus-truck victim. Possible flail chest injury.

Hurrying after the only man Tamara had been intimate with in years, her gaze automatically scanned Conor's longish black hair at the back of his neck, remembering how she'd run her fingers through the glossy waves. That had been then. Today was a whole new ball game. Learning she was carrying his baby was going to knock Conor off his impeccable stride.

Tamara heard the paramedic begin to give Conor her report on their latest stat one patient, and pulled on her professional face, straightened her back into its now usual, though false, don't-fool-with-me, ramrod-straight line and pushed aside any thoughts not related to work.

'Impact to the chest from the steering wheel, suspected broken ribs and perforated lungs.'

Conor interrupted the woman. 'Tamara, take over debrief. I'm getting this guy into Resus and the radiology technician onto him now.' Calm belied the urgency of Conor's statement; the only giveaway to his concern a thickening of that mouth-watering drawl. He was already rushing the stretcher towards Resus, a second ambulance officer with him moving as fast.

Time was running out if their man had a flail chest. With broken ribs tearing holes in the lungs on every breath, the guy would simply run out of oxygen in very little time.

'How long since the accident happened?' she demanded of the paramedic, worried about the man's chances of survival.

'Approximately fifteen minutes ago. Just around the corner on Grafton Road. We were already on the road, heading to another accident, when the call came through. It was a load-and-go the moment we figured out what might be his major injury.'

'Good on you for not hanging around, checking him

out.' Seemed something was on their patient's side. 'What else have you got?'

As the paramedic listed the other injuries Jimmy Crowe had sustained, Tamara couldn't help sighing with relief. She was going to be busy for the next hour, so her mind would stay shut down on everything else.

'Tamara, we need oxygen happening,' Conor called as she ran into Resus. 'ASAP.'

'Onto it.' Tamara shoved the paperwork into another nurse's hands. 'Kelli, can you read these obs out to Conor?' Reaching for the gas, she mentally crossed her fingers they weren't too late and that some oxygen would do its job.

She and Kelli worked in unison with Conor to get Jimmy's bleeding and breathing under some sort of control. A cannula was slid into the left arm to allow for essential fluids to enter the man's bloodstream.

Michael, a registrar, joined them. 'A steering-wheel injury?'

Conor nodded. 'Yes.'

Tamara wiped blood from the man's mouth. 'This could back up the lung-damage theory.'

'Stand back, everyone,' the radiology tech called from behind his portable unit. *Whizz, click, whizz.* Angles were changed, more images taken. Even before he'd finished Conor demanded, 'What've we got?'

'Give me a minute.'

'We haven't got a minute.'

Tamara understood Conor's impatience. Their patient's life depended on what the X-rays showed.

The images appeared almost immediately on the screen and Conor studied them with the intensity of a specialist determined not to lose his patient. 'Fractures to the right side of his rib cage but no ribs pushed in at the front. There's some displacement at the front, and two ribs have broken off the sternum, but they're not causing further damage to the lungs.'

From beside him Tamara also peered at the images. The tightness in her shoulders did not ease. 'I think our man's very lucky.'

'On count one, yes. But from my observations so far there's probably a skull fracture, likewise with the right elbow, where, going by the amount of blood leakage, the artery is torn, plus internal injuries to deal with.' Conor had already called for someone to get onto the lab to come and take a blood sample for cross-match. He turned to the guy from Radiology. 'I need pictures of his pelvis and arms while you're at it. Flick them all straight through to the radiologist.'

'No problem.'

'His spleen's damaged,' Conor reported later after a call from the radiology department. 'Wonder what caused that? And the other injuries below the ribs,' he pondered aloud as he snatched up the phone again. 'I'm getting the surgical team on standby up to speed.'

'The corner of the other vehicle must've pushed the side of the car inwards,' Tamara commented.

'How's that oxygen flow?' Conor demanded as he held the phone to his ear. 'What's his sat level?'

Everyone worked quickly and thoroughly, doing their damnedest to save the man's life. When they finally stepped away to let the orderly take Jimmy to Theatre, where surgeons were scrubbed and waiting, Tamara felt exhaustion roll through her. 'That was crazy.' But what they were used to. Except she didn't usually feel so tired afterwards.

Tiredness *and* nausea. Not normal for her. But they were for pregnancy. The towel she was unfolding dropped to the floor. It was so unfair it was incomprehensible. Oh, like life hadn't been inconsiderate before? Hadn't blown up in her face in the past?

On the far side of the room Conor was talking through a yawn. 'I hate impact injuries. They're often extreme and messy, let alone hard to stabilise.' Why was he tired? Had a busy weekend between the sheets, had he?

A twinge of regret tightened her already tight stomach. Jealousy didn't suit her, and was irrelevant as they were only friends and colleagues. Conor liked the ladies, nothing new there. She'd been quick to walk away after that fantastic night in his bed, being wary of any more involvement with him. Even then her heart had sent her a warning: *Beware, Conor's dangerous to your determination to remain single.*

She watched him rubbing his lower back as he stretched up onto his toes, swivelling his neck left then right. His gaze caught hers as he continued, 'Vehicles of all kinds are so damned dangerous.'

Her breath hitched in her throat as she locked eyes with him. A look like this one had led to her predicament. A night on the town with colleagues and *kapow!* One of those lingering, across-heads-of-people-dancing looks and she'd known they'd have to connect up. And reciprocal knowledge had been blinking out at her from Conor's eyes. No denying something had to happen between them. And it had. Her mouth watered at the memories of the hottest night she'd ever experienced. And he was looking at her like that now. Her gut tightened. It would be so easy to follow through on the promise in those eyes.

Problem. They were at work. It wasn't happening again. She was about to turn his world upside down. How many more reasons did she need?

'Hello, Tamara. Anyone home?' Conor waved at her,

stopping those distracting thoughts. Not that he looked any more comfortable than she was.

What had they been talking about? Vehicles and danger. 'Enough to put me off driving.' Tamara dragged her eyes forward, away from the promise, avoiding that toned body, and focused on the bed she needed to strip. The muscles his scrubs were hiding were lean and strong and sexy.

She'd been rambling on about driving when she didn't own a car. That eye-lock had a lot to answer for. 'Being bowled off my bike would be a bigger mess, I reckon.' The bike on her back porch that had a thick layer of dust covering it and spiders' nests between the spokes of the wheels sitting on flat tyres.

'You ever going to ride that thing again?' Kelli asked with a hint of amusement from the other side of the bed.

Not in the foreseeable future. Her hand touched her tummy before she realised where she was and jerked it away. People around here had eyes in the back of their skulls. 'I doubt it. I'm such a wimp. Since that day I rode into a grass-covered ditch and got tossed into the field, I keep thinking about splatting onto the road.' She shivered. The media had been chasing her for a comment on her ex's latest crime that had been exposed. It was lucky she'd got away with three stitches in her arm where a broken bottle hidden in the grass had sliced her. 'I know a warning when I see one.'

Not with Conor, she hadn't. His easy manner and take-me-or-leave-me attitude had added to the compelling physical need he'd stirred up within her over that dance floor. He'd been the first man since Peter. The first kiss, first sex, first sleepover. Sort of like getting back in the saddle, only more frightening because she'd understood how hard the fall could be.

At least with Conor it had only been about the great sex,

and one night had not led to others. In fact, he'd seemed relieved when she'd leapt out of bed the following morning, hauled on her clothes, and declared, thanks, but got to go. He hadn't seen the fear of wanting more from him that she'd struggled to hold at bay until she'd got away. The fear made harder to hide when he'd done an about-face and invited her to breakfast at a classy café near his apartment. Almost as if her rejection had piqued his interest. When, in desperation, she'd declined, he'd insisted on walking her to the bus stop. All part of his charm, and utterly dangerous in its temptation.

'Incoming severe asthma attack,' the triage nurse called as she slammed the phone back in place. 'ETA ten minutes.'

'No rest for the wicked.' Conor grinned. 'Or even the slightly bad.'

'We can't complain that the day's dragging,' Tamara retorted. Her day was taking for ever to tick by, yet at the same time three o'clock was charging at her full speed. How would Conor react? Would he storm out, shouting that she was a liar or a con artist? Or would he pat her on the head and say good luck and goodbye?

'What is up with you today? You're very distracted.' Conor studied her from his six-foot-plus height. 'Come to think of it, you're looking peaky.'

'I'm fine,' she snapped, and headed to a cubicle where she could hear a middle-aged woman with a suspected broken ankle groaning. Peaky? Right. Of course she was peaky. She'd tossed up her breakfast that morning, hadn't she? At least it'd happened before she left home and not on the bus, or, worse, not here where some nosy parker would notice quicker than wildfire ignited dry tinder and come up with the wrong cause. Or the right one.

'Tamara, I want you on the asthma with me,' Conor called after her.

'No problem,' she lied. *Ask someone else.*

'In a better mood.'

Tamara nearly leapt into the air. She hadn't heard him coming closer. 'Don't sneak up on me,' she growled as her heart thumped loud enough for the whole department to hear.

'Whoa.' His hands were up, palms towards her. 'Maybe you need to take a quick coffee break. Get some caffeine into your system. Something's got your knickers in a twist and it's not a good look in ED.'

He was right. When wasn't he? On a long, raggedy in-drawn suck of air she managed, 'Sorry. I had a restless night. Seems it's catching up with me.' As if she could have slept when the truth had been leaching into her mind, pushing aside her dreams, taunting her. No wonder her head was beginning to pound like there was a band of bongo drummers in there. She never did well on less than eight hours' sleep. Something she'd planned on getting used to once she started her medical training.

Now she was readjusting, learning the new phrase— once she became a mother.

'Your mood anything to do with what you want to talk to me about?'

Too shrewd for your own good, Dr Maguire.

'No. Yes. Sort of.'

'Bring me a coffee when you get yours, will you?'

In other words, she wasn't getting away without a caffeine fix. Sorry, baby. Don't take any on board, or you'll be buzzing all afternoon. 'Three sugars?' She arched an eyebrow at him.

'For you, not me.' He flipped a smile in her direction

before reaching for another patient form, that earlier tiredness now tugging at his mouth.

Damn that smile. It could undo all her resolve to be firm with him. 'Looks like you need the caffeine more than I do,' Tamara muttered as she headed for the kitchenette. Tea for her. It might be less aggressive on her system. See, getting used to there being a baby growing inside.

Her knees gave out on her and she buckled against the wall as very real fear overcame her. Her dream was going up in smoke before she'd even pushed 'send' on that application. Becoming a mother was not part of the plan, had only been a remote, 'not likely to happen in this lifetime' kind of dream. But not any more. Not in her current situation. How was she going to cope? It wasn't as though she'd had a good role model in her mother. While Dad had been the steady influence, Mum had always been a little off kilter, doing things without thought to time or place or other people. Like hopping on a flight to Melbourne for the fashion show and not telling Dad where she was until she'd landed. Dad had shrugged, said that's your mother for you, and taken her out to dinner at a five-star restaurant. She'd been six at the time. Which parent would she follow? She knew which one she wanted to be like, but wasn't sure of her capabilities.

'Tamara? What's going on?'

Conor could be so nosy. She shuffled her body up the wall until she stood upright, not quite ramrod straight, and eyeballed him. 'Having a wee kip on the way to get those drinks.'

'You think you should be at work? You're not exactly on form today.'

'Have I made any mistakes? Looked incapable of doing my job?'

'Not yet.' Conor studied her for a long moment. No

heated connection going on now. 'Take thirty. Get something to eat to go with that coffee.' Her face must've given her away because his hand went up, palm out. 'No argument.'

When he took her arm and led her into the tiny space that was the staff kitchenette she had no choice other than to go with him. Putting up a fight was a waste of time and energy that was best saved for other more important issues.

'Here.' Conor removed a brown paper bag from a cupboard and placed it on the bench. 'Cheese scone from the café. Get it down you.' Then he reached for the coffee.

A warning rose from her tense gut. No way. Food would have to wait. 'Th-thanks. Tea for me.' And this was the woman who had taken control of her life and refused to let anyone or anything tip her off track again? Tamara reached for the bag, tore it open and broke off a tiny corner of the scone. *Shut up, stomach. Whose side are you on, anyway?* And she popped the morsel into her mouth and chewed. And chewed. Swallowed. *Take that.* She took another small bite, and locked eyes with Conor. 'Just what I needed,' she agreed around a wave of relief that her stomach was supporting her. However briefly. For now she was back on track.

'I'll hand that asthma over to one of the junior doctors, then we'll take our drinks to my office and have that talk you asked for.'

'What? Now?' She tipped sideways, grabbed at the bench. 'It can wait.' *I'm not ready.*

'Something's up and it's affecting you. Best we sort it and get on with the day. Finish making those drinks, will you?' Conor shot out the door, leaving her shaking.

On autopilot she spooned coffee into one mug, dropped a tea bag into another, added sugar and boiling water to both. Stirred. *It's too late to do a runner. Time to face the facts.*

'Ready? Good.' Conor swooped back into the small space, picked up both full mugs in one hand and took her elbow in the other. 'Let's go.'

And then they were there, Conor's office door clicking shut behind her, and the air all hot and heavy. Tamara sank onto the closest chair, gripped her hands between her knees and stared at the floor. She should've dug into the back of her wardrobe and found something half-decent to wear for this, instead of looking like the frump she hid behind. But then he'd have known something was up.

She heard the mugs being placed on the desk, Conor's chair being pulled out, his knee clicking as he sat down. She felt his eyes on her, his bewilderment boring into her. Her skin chilled, and the moisture evaporated from her mouth.

Slowly lifting her head, she nearly leapt up and ran. There was so much concern radiating out at her from across the desk it undermined all the lessons on men she'd learned from her ex. Could Conor care about her that much?

'Start at the beginning.' Conor's soft voice flowed over her, tightening already tight muscles and jangling nerve endings.

There was no beginning. No ending. Only the facts. Her spine couldn't straighten to ramrod straight. Her tongue felt too big for her mouth. Her heart squeezed in on itself so hard pain shot out in all directions. 'I'm pregnant.'

He rocked backwards in his chair, those beautiful eyes widening with disbelief. Or was it shock? She couldn't read him clearly. Gone was the open-faced, cheerful, friendly man everyone adored.

Might as well go for broke, put it all out there. In a strangled whisper, she told him, 'You're the baby's father.'

Then she waited for the axe to fall. And waited and waited. The silence was stifling. The walls came closer, squeezing the heavy air around her, suffocating her.

Say something, Conor.

CHAPTER TWO

'I'm PREGNANT.' The words ricocheted from wall to wall.

Conor slammed back in his seat as all the air in his lungs spewed into the room. The silence was deafening. As if everyone in the hospital was holding their collective breath.

'You're the baby's father.'

Tell me this isn't true. But Tamara looked certain. Apprehensive, but definitely sure. There was no colour in her cheeks, no warmth in her eyes, and her hands were rubbing her arms like they were cold. 'You can't be. I used condoms.' Rule number one: when indulging in sex, use protection. No exceptions.

'I am, and you did.'

No, no, no. He leapt to his feet, an oath spilling across his lips. 'You're saying one was faulty?' He saw his disbelief drill into her, wanted to regret his words, but couldn't quite. She mustn't be pregnant. Not with *his* child.

Tamara pulled back, her eyes locked on him. 'Faulty, torn in use, I have no idea. I only know that I haven't had a period since that weekend, and there was a blue line on the test stick.' She gulped. 'On both sticks.'

'Making certain, were you? Crossing the "t"s and dotting the "i"s?' So like Tamara, he'd laugh if there was anything humorous about this. A chill was spreading through him. She wasn't lying. It wasn't a sick joke. Not that she'd ever do that. It was just that… It was impossible to believe.

Because he didn't want to. He'd been running from getting involved for the last fourteen years. Hell, he'd come all the way down to New Zealand to keep the yearning for love and family at bay. To stand alone, not get close to anyone. Showed how much he knew. Seemed life had always been going to catch up with him, regardless of what he did.

'There's a lot at stake.' There was a quiver in Tamara's voice that rattled him.

And pricked his heart. *Don't go there*. He wasn't available. Conor opened up to the chill ramping through him, let it into his voice box. 'Sure is. When did you do the tests?'

'Friday. Then Saturday.'

Conor felt his face tighten, worked at softening his facial muscles. Failed. 'You could've said something sooner. You've got my phone number.' Genuine anger was moving in, heating his cheeks, deflecting the chill.

'I could have, yes.' Tamara swallowed, started again. 'But I didn't want to believe it. Telling you makes it irrefutably real.'

'You were in denial.' That he could understand. About where he was right now.

'Totally. I have—' *Gasp.* Her hands clenched tight on her elbows. 'I *had* plans, and being pregnant is upending everything. Again. I've worked so hard to be in charge of my future.'

What did she mean by again? And being in charge of herself? Wasn't everybody? 'You don't want the baby?' he snapped. How did that make him feel? Relieved? Not at all. Really? Who the hell knew? Not him. He charged for the door, reached for the handle to haul it open. Stopped. Spun around to face her, rose up and down on his toes as he waited for her reply to his telling question.

'I never said that,' she said sharply. 'Or implied it.'

'Just checking.' *Sounding like a heel, boyo.* Now, there was a surprise. His head was full to the brim with questions, denials, longings, anger—every blasted emotion under the sun. Name it, it was there. 'I don't know you well enough to read your mind.'

Tamara fixed him with a glare. 'Then take this on board. I won't be going to university next year after all, and I so wanted to become a doctor. Instead I'm having a baby. Then I'm going to be a mother, something I know next to nothing about.' She stared at him, imploring him to understand. 'I don't want to be like my mother. She believed nannies were put on earth so she could go to charity meetings and play mediocre golf.'

The bitterness colouring those words was almost tangible and Conor wanted to wipe it away, make her feel better. So he remained by the door. Start doing that and who knew what would happen next. They had a lot to get through over the coming weeks and any out-of-the-ordinary moves like that would only turn everything murky. He had to be aloof, separate. 'I'd have said she did a great job with you.' There, honest but uninvolved.

Tamara snarled, 'Don't talk about something you know nothing about.'

Ouch. He'd hit a painful point, for sure. 'Fair enough.' He strode back to his chair, dropped into it and banged his feet on the desktop. His hands gripped together under his chin as he studied Tamara. Looking for what? He wasn't sure.

'There's nothing fair about any of this,' she retorted.

He couldn't agree more. But what he said was, 'You have no idea.'

'About what?' she asked in a rare belligerent tone.

'I can't have children.'

'Wrong. You are having one next year. In April, I reckon. It's no one else's.'

'I am not accusing you of lying to me, Tamara.'

She lurched, as though stabbed by pain. Her hands clenched even tighter. But she kept her head high and those cocoa-coloured eyes fixed on him. 'Then I don't understand.'

'I can't have children. It's as simple as that.'

Someone knocking on the door had Conor hauling his feet off the table quick fast. 'Go away. I'm busy,' he yelled in frustration.

They both held their breaths until it became apparent whoever was out there had taken his advice.

Tamara asked quietly, 'You can't? Or won't?'

Back to the elephant. She knew next to nothing about him, and he wasn't about to let his tongue go crazy filling in the gaps. Though there was one detail he'd have to reveal. His feet hit the floor in an instant, and his head spun as he came upright. Not now. Not today.

'Conor?' Not so quiet.

'Either way, it makes no difference.'

Tamara's eyes narrowed. 'If there are things I need to know for my baby's sake then tell me.'

He moved away from the desk abruptly, his chair flung back against the wall. His hands went to his hips, held tight. 'All my adult life I've actively avoided this exact moment. Yet here it is, staring me down.' Commitment with a capital C.

'Don't you like children? You're always amazing with them in the department, teasing and fun, easing their distress. I wouldn't have believed you were faking it.' She paused, and when he didn't answer she continued. 'We need to talk, about a lot of things. Seems you've got issues. Which means I do too. I need to know what they are, Conor. For our child's sake, if nothing else.'

'What I need right now is some air. This office is stuffy. I'll see you back at work shortly.' Pulling the door open, he stepped right up against Michael's extended hand.

'I was about to knock,' the registrar muttered, dropping his hand quickly. 'We've got a situation and you're both needed. Urgently.'

'I'm on my break.' Conor hauled the brakes on his motor mouth, breathed deep. 'Sorry, start again. What situation?'

I need to get away from here, from Tamara and the distress in those serious eyes. I need to work out what's just happened. Have I spent fourteen years being deliberately solo for nothing?

He felt movement beside him, heard Tamara ask, in a voice that didn't sound a lot stronger than his, 'What is it, Michael?'

'I've just got off the phone from Ambulance Headquarters. All hell's about to break out. There's been an accident involving a busload of children.'

Saved by the phone. Conor started down the corridor towards the centre of the department, and swore. He didn't really wish harm on those kids so he could avoid facing up to Tamara's news. News that at the moment had to go on hold. 'Continue.'

'A school bus has rolled off the motorway on-ramp in Newmarket. There are many serious casualties.' The registrar's voice slowed, dropped an octave. 'And some fatalities.'

Conor saw the precise moment the reality of what he'd reported to them hit Michael. The guy's eyes widened, and his body sagged a little. Something like his own re-action to Tamara's news. Laying a hand on his shoulder, he said, 'Okay, get everyone together and I'll outline how we go about this.'

'They're all waiting for you and Tamara at the desk.' Michael's voice cracked. 'This is huge.'

'We'll manage by breaking it down into components.' Conor was already busy drawing up a mental list of people to call, jobs to do, equipment to check over. The moment he stood in front of his team he wasted no time. 'Firstly, no one's going home at three.' The clock showed two thirty-five. He glanced at Tamara, who'd moved in beside Kelli.

Horror and despair for what they would shortly be dealing with filled her eyes. All of the previous distress about their own personal situation had been shoved aside. He nodded at her. Very impressive. She'd been ahead of him.

A tall, blond-haired man stepped into the area. 'What's up?'

'Mac.' Conor nodded at the head of the evening shift as he joined them. 'We're about to receive multiple stat one junior patients from a bus accident.' He quickly added the few details he had. 'You should take over right from the start. It's going to be your roster.'

Mac shook his head. 'No, you carry on, get things rolling. Your team's all here, mine is yet to arrive.'

It made sense, and in some ways Conor was pleased. He preferred leading from the front, but that also meant there was a very long night ahead. He turned to Michael. 'When can we expect the first patient?' Patient, not child. It helped him keep his distance a little bit. But only until the first victim arrived. Then his heart would break for the child and his or her family. Every time he had to tell a parent bad news he saw his mother, distraught, inconsolable as she kissed his brother goodbye before the funeral.

Michael's voice came through. 'Coms couldn't tell me times or numbers. She said it's absolute chaos out there. Because we're closest we get the first, most urgent cases, then they'll start feeding out to other hospitals.'

'First we need to clear as many beds as we can. Michael, what've we got?'

'One lad about to have his arm put in plaster. A woman with unidentified head pain awaiting lab results. There are also two stat five patients in the waiting room.'

'Kelli, take the boy, get him fixed up and on his way home. Michael, see if the general ward can accommodate the head-pain patient and let them follow up on her blood results as they come in.'

'Onto it.'

'Tamara.' When had she come to stand next to him? Like she was offering support? He should've felt her there, but he wasn't used to looking to someone else for comfort or sharing. He looked into that steady dark gaze and knew he was glad she was with him. For now they were on the same page, despite the chasm yawning between them. A baby. Longing unfurled slowly deep inside. Family. The thing he'd denied himself for life. Even when he'd desperately wanted one. Was this the universe's way of saying he was wrong?

An elbow nudging his arm reminded him of what he was meant to be thinking about. Nothing to do with babies. 'Right, Tamara.'

'What do you want me to do?' she asked, clearly weighing up all that had to be done before their first little patient came through those wide doors from the ambulance bays.

'In the waiting room, those stat fives. Send the man with the possible sprained ankle straight to Radiology. I'll let them know he's coming and why the hurry.'

'Right.' She made to move away.

She was obviously not as distracted as he was, then. This woman was the ultimate professional, hiding behind that impenetrable façade, letting nothing personal affect her work. He'd only once seen her mask come down completely. *Whoa. Do not go there.* 'Wait. The man with a constant bleeding nose can go over the way to the emergency doctors' clinic.'

'He's going to love that,' Tamara muttered as she reached to pick up the patient notes.

'Explain the situation. He'll get just as good care there, and certainly a lot quicker. Tell Reception to send people to medical centres where possible after the triage nurse has assessed them. Once those kids start arriving no one else is going to get a look in unless they're stat one.'

'Give me the easy job, why don't you?' There was no acid in her retort. Maybe it wasn't a retort, considering the lift of those full lips into something resembling a tentative smile. A Tamara smile—rarely given, and never over-eager—was something to hold onto.

Warmth flooded him because of that smile. Warmth that only Tamara seemed capable of giving him at a deeper level than just fun and enjoyment. He found her a smile in return, and drank in her surprise. Hopefully she didn't know how she affected him when he wasn't being careful, which around her was becoming more and more difficult. Hence why he'd applied for a job in Sydney, hopefully starting next month.

Staff from the next shift were wandering in one at a time. A low hum of whispers told the newcomers what they were about to deal with. Conor looked at Mac, who said, 'Pretty much everyone's here so carry on. You've started the process.'

Facing the eager faces, Conor told the nurses and registrars, 'All of you, double check we're ready and prepared for every eventuality. You know what to do. Treat this as you would any stat one coming through the door, but know there's going to be a seemingly endless stream. It will come to an end, I assure you, but there'll be moments when you doubt that.' He paused to let his words sink in, then said, 'I'll be on the phone, putting people around the hospital on standby, but interrupt me if you find there's a problem anywhere. There are going to be double ups amongst you but, believe me, you will all be required.'

Mac took over allocating jobs while Conor punched in the direct dial number for the theatre manager. 'Sister, we have a situation.' He quickly brought her up to speed and then left her to get on with cancelling surgeries and getting theatres prepared for the influx due any moment.

Theatres, done. Running through a mental list of who he had to notify, he punched in the next number. Radiology, then surgeons and other specialists, blood bank.

'Everyone's busy so I can take some of those calls.' Mac stood in front of him, phone in hand. 'Who's next?'

'Orthopaedics.'

Together they worked systematically through the list, the whole time Conor watching the minutes ticking by, feeling the tension building in himself and the department as the doors from the ambulance bay remained firmly shut. He slammed the phone down on his final call. 'Come on. Where are these kids? The odds aren't great if they don't get here *now*.'

Mac shook his head. 'We're organised, ready and waiting. But, yeah, where the hell are those children?'

The buzzer screamed, cutting through the air, sounding louder and more urgent than normal. Instant silence fell across the department and every head turned towards those doors.

Conor drew a breath. 'Okay, everyone, good luck. I know you'll do your damnedest.' And then some.

As he took a step his gaze slid from the doors to Tamara. She was pale, but ramrod straight, and her nod in his direction was assured. Then she was moving to let in their first patient, and Conor was right beside her.

'Jamie Johnson, eight years old, severe concussion.'

Then the flood started.

'Carole Miller, facial injuries, nine years old.'

'Toby Crawford, eight years old, unconscious, suspected skull fracture, internal injuries.'

Once it began the line of trauma victims was continuous and the severity of the cases presenting mind-numbing. A brief gap ninety minutes in gave everyone time to nearly catch up before the second wave of children arrived. These kids were in worse condition than the initial ones because they'd taken longer to be extricated from the wreckage that had once been a bus.

'We need blood here.' Tamara was beckoning to the lab technician to take a sample for cross-match from her patient prior to his surgery for a severed foot.

'And here,' Kelli called from the next resus unit, where a tiny lad with a broken kneecap and torn artery lay whimpering in a fog of morphine.

Conor called to Tamara, 'Get the orthopaedic surgeon in here.'

The phone was at her ear immediately as she hadn't put it down from her last urgent call. For a brief moment they locked eyes and he felt a surge of adrenalin. It was like she was his other half. The calm, self-assured nurse who now had him under control and as calm as she was. The woman carrying his baby. Conor's gut clenched. Baby. Child. Accidents. Death and destruction. Forget calm. What if something like this happened to their child? What—?

'Here.' Tamara shoved the phone at him and instantly replaced his hands with hers on their small patient's leg to continue pressing on a pad staunching the blood flow that had restarted while they'd been investigating his injuries.

Conor swallowed down the fear and said into the phone, 'Kay, we've got a lad whose left foot has been severed.' As he rattled off details he refused to think about how the loss of a foot would affect a young child. Instead he concentrated on Tamara as she bent over the boy, whispering sweet nothings to him even when there wasn't a chance in hell the boy heard a word. This was Tamara at her best. Calming.

That night in his bed she'd been the antithesis of calm.

Conor slammed the phone back on the hook. *Concentrate, man.* He called, 'Orderly,' and returned to the lad's side. 'Obs? How's that oxygen flow?'

Mam, how did you survive watching Sebastian die?

Conor's heart stopped. Slashing his forearm across his eyes, he stared at the boy before him. Life was so unfair. But he wasn't going to let this kid die.

Bright lights flashed in the department, temporarily blinding Conor. 'What the…?'

'Get out of here,' Tamara snarled. 'Conor,' she yelled. 'We need Security. Yesterday.'

Conor blinked, saw rage fill Tamara's face, her eyes, as she stalked past him towards a man pointing a camera in the direction of their patient.

'The media?' *Tell me I'm wrong.* 'How the hell did you get in here?' he demanded of the man, anger now running in his veins too.

'Like they always do, by pushing people aside as if they have a right to.' Tamara was shaking.

He placed a hand on her shoulder. 'Ignore him. Our patient needs us.' Where were those security guys?

The camera flashed again, and Tamara stepped away from it, her face contorted with a mix of anger and hopelessness. Then two guys in uniform were hauling the cameraman away none too gently.

Conor turned Tamara back to their case. 'Don't think about it. Save it for later. You're needed with our lad at the moment.'

Her body shuddered as she drew a breath, and she slapped the back of her glove-covered hand across her cheeks. 'They have no respect for anyone.'

'Tam, focus now.'

'Don't call me Tam,' she snapped, but at least her spine straightened and all her focus returned to where it was meant to be.

He worked with Tamara, stabilising and checking blood flow, oxygen, getting the boy ready for surgery. Then his patient was gone, onto the next phase of being put back together, though for the boy that would be a long process.

Tamara's eyes were chilly and giving nothing away as she stretched her back, pushing her breasts up. His mouth dried. Then he recalled some comments made about her when he'd first started here. Something about how the media were always waiting to pounce if she so much as breathed out of order. She had history with them, but he'd never asked what it was about, figuring it was none of his business.

Now he wanted to take them all down in a bloody thrashing for upsetting Tamara.

A little girl arrived before them.

'Nine years old, suspected fractures to both arms and legs, and possibly ribs.' A nurse from the nightshift read the details as Conor nodded to the X-ray tech.

The thrashing would have to wait.

As would thinking about that baby.

The hours disappeared in a haze of anguish and despair. Children came through ED, some staying longer than others before moving on to Theatre, or, for the lucky ones, to the children's ward with plaster casts or multitudes of stitches.

Finally, 'We're all done.' Mac appeared from the adjoining resus unit, looking like he'd been living a nightmare for hours. Which he had. They all had.

It was over. Air leaked from Conor like a puncture as the tension that had been with him from the moment Michael had told them what they were in for softened. 'I didn't know they could fit so many children on one bus.' The exhaustion that'd been beating him up earlier in the afternoon returned at full throttle. 'Glad that's done.' Except there were parents throughout the hospital dealing with their worst nightmares.

Parents. Closing his eyes, he rubbed them with his thumbs, and was confronted with an image of Mam letting herself in through the front door, shoulders drooped, knees buckling. Those laughing eyes he'd looked for on waking every morning of his four short years had been dulled with pain and anguish. Her arms had shaken as she'd clung to him. He hadn't recognised her voice as she'd croaked, 'Sebastian and Daddy are in heaven, my love.' And there had begun the rest of his life.

'I've never dealt with anything like it.' Mac rolled his neck left then right.

'What?'

'Go home, Conor. Get a beer in you and hit the sack.'

Looking around, Conor couldn't find Tamara. He stumbled. 'Where is everyone?'

Tam, did you cope? Really? Behind that mask, are you okay?

Mac was muttering, 'I sent day shift home half an hour ago. They were shattered after already working a shift, and I figured my team could handle the remainder of cases. Not that they're in much better shape.'

'It's going to be a long night for them.' What was left of it.

Mac gave him a rueful smile. 'You sure knew how to cope with the situation.'

'For all the wrong reasons, unfortunately.' The wall clock read nine twenty. He wouldn't have been surprised if it was after midnight. As it was, he'd be back on duty all too soon. With that thought his mind filled with the urgent need to get out of there while he could still walk. 'I'm gone.'

Home. A shower. Bed.

Tamara.

Now that you're coming down from the high we've all been on for endless hours, are you looking all peaky and worried again?

She'd be beyond exhausted now that she had pregnancy to contend with as well.

I hope you're all right. That my baby is doing okay.

CHAPTER THREE

Tamara huddled against the bench in her kitchen, waiting for the toaster to pop. Wet hair hung down her back. Blow-drying it would take energy she didn't have. Tomorrow it would stick out in all directions but right now she didn't care. All she wanted was to eat something fast before slipping between the clean sheets she'd put on the bed that morning. To fall asleep and forget all the horrors of the day.

Those poor little kids, broken, in agony, some damaged for ever. The parents' distress had been equally harrowing. Not something she'd have considered from a parent's perspective until that thin blue line had entered her life. Never before had she seen such despair, so much shock, all at once.

The day the fraud squad had turned up at her family home had been shocking, but in a very different way; certainly not life-threatening, only life-changing. Back then, the press she had been used to, following her around to photograph her latest outfit or hairstyle, or who she'd dined with and where, had turned on her. Painted her the same black shade as Peter. From that day on she and the media had come to a mutual understanding. They disliked each other; a far cry from the fawning she'd grown up knowing and enjoying. These days, loath to attract attention of any kind, she no longer wore supermodel clothes or spent a fortune on make-up and hair. Nowadays she hid behind dull and duller.

A sigh escaped. What a day. And she'd thought telling Conor about their baby had been difficult. It had been a breeze compared to what those poor parents were dealing with.

Ding-dong. The doorbell was loud in the quiet space.

Her neck cricked painfully when her head snapped up. Who was here at this hour? She didn't have visitors at any hour. Staring at her bedraggled reflection in the microwave door, she hoped whoever was out there would take the hint and go away.

Ding-dong.

Pulling the belt of her bathrobe tight, she took another moment to stare at the image gleaming back at her. Whoever it was, they'd soon take a hike when they saw her looking like something hauled out of a dumpster.

Ding-dong.

Persistent. 'Yes, yes, I'm coming,' she muttered as she gave in. Opening the front door, a gasp escaped her. 'Conor.' Might have known, considering the persistence aspect.

'Did you check to see who was out here before you opened the door?' he growled.

She hadn't given it a thought. 'Hang on.' She made to close the door and peek through the eye-hole just to wind Conor up. How else to deal with him when she could barely remember her own name?

He was too quick for her, splaying his hand on the door to keep it open. 'Can I come in?'

Don't tell me we're going to discuss our baby now.

She'd be at a huge disadvantage, her brain only functioning on low. Yet she stepped back, breathed him in as he passed. Her body succumbed to the scent of man with an overlay of antiseptic. 'You've come straight from the hospital?' she finally managed.

'I wanted to make sure you'd got home all right and was coping with what went down in ED today.'

Of course she was. And wasn't. 'There'll probably be some nightmares, but I'm fine.' He cared enough to check on her? When he had to be feeling as shattered as she did? Raising her eyes to his, she found concern and something she couldn't interpret fixed on her. 'Thank you,' she whispered around the lump suddenly clogging her throat. When was the last time a man—anyone, for that matter—had shown her such care? No one since her father had become ill with the dementia that had taken him from her. Not even Peter had managed to pull on a mask that had suggested he'd been genuinely concerned for her any time. One of the lesser reasons he was now her ex. 'Thanks,' she repeated.

'Come here.' Conor wrapped her up in a strong yet gentle hug, held her against his warm length and lowered his chin to the top of her wet head. 'It's been a huge day.'

Tamara's arms lifted to his waist without any input from her brain. She snuggled her face into his chest. 'Massive,' she agreed.

'You were amazing with your little patients. So caring, understanding, unflappable. I've worked with a lot of nurses and you are one of the best.' A large, warm hand ran soft, soothing circles over her back. Slowly, slowly, the tension ebbed away, leaving her feeling comfortable with Conor.

Seriously? Oh, boy. That made her feel so good. 'I could say the same back to you.' And mean it as much as she believed he meant it.

'So…' Conor hesitated. 'You're okay now you've come down off the high brought on by the adrenalin rush today cranked up?'

'I'm shattered so I don't want to discuss our baby and how we're going to deal with this situation tonight. I don't believe I can be as focused as I need to be for that.' Conor holding her like this made her feel as though she could tell him anything, open up to him, explain how she hoped their future—their baby's future—would unfold. And probably give too much of herself away.

'I came around to make sure you were all right. I also needed to hear you mention the pregnancy again. It's been a blur from the moment Michael knocked on my office door.'

Leaning back in his arms, she gazed up at him. 'We are going to have a baby.'

'Right.' Those blue eyes locked on hers, and this time the electricity that often flowed between them was quiet. More of an accepting, compliant force. But he'd have his own agenda. Everyone did. While talking about her training to become a doctor, he'd mentioned his plans for the coming years, starting with an application he'd sent in for a position in an emergency department in Sydney Hospital.

Had he heard whether he'd got the job? She tensed. Where would that leave her and the baby? Free to raise her child as she chose? Or would he demand she follow him across the Tasman? If Conor turned out to be as manipulative as Peter had then she wished him to Siberia. Neither would she be following. Her exhausted muscles contracted some more. There was a lot to learn about this man before she could begin to make any plans for her and baby's future.

'Easy does it,' Conor murmured above her. 'Relax. We can put off in-depth and meaningful conversations for another day.'

Sure thing. She tried to pull out of those compelling arms. Conor simply tightened his hold, keeping her spread against him. Giving in, she went with the moment, absorbed his strength, his warmth, him.

Who knew how long they stood there, holding one another? All Tamara understood was that she didn't want to move ever again. She'd temporarily found her safe place in Conor's arms, and to pull away would sever whatever had brought them together. To move apart would bring back all the doubts and questions, would waken her up to the reality that she didn't know her baby's father well enough to put their needs in his hands. Or to trust him to do what was right for her. At the moment she was beyond leaving his arms, no matter what the consequences.

Finally Conor lifted his head and tilted it back to look down into her eyes. 'I've ordered Thai. It should arrive any minute. I had to make sure you ate something more than a piece of toast.'

'How'd you know that's what I'd have?'

'It was a guess. Might know you better than you think.' He smiled, a slow cautious lifting of those clever lips. 'Can I take a shower before we eat?'

'Help yourself.' Or should she be kicking him out? She was still edgy about him being here.

Conor dropped his arms. 'Thanks, Tam.'

'Don't call me Tam.' It was an automatic response. She didn't deserve her dad's pet name any more.

His eyes widened but all he asked was, 'Where's the bathroom?'

'In the interests of saving you what little energy you've probably got left, follow me.' As if her flat needed a map. 'Here. Help yourself to towels under the basin. I'll pull on some proper clothes and warm the oven for the Thai so you don't have to rush.'

Conor ran his knuckles lightly over her cheek. 'Stay

like you are. I'm only here for a short while and you'll be wanting to head to bed as soon as I've gone.'

Bed and Conor in the same thought should've cranked up her desire levels. They didn't. Right now she was all out of anything but the need to eat and sleep. And by the exhaustion rippling off Conor he wasn't any keener to get naked with her either. 'Okay.' Anyway, something as intimate as sex wasn't happening while they were grappling with this new situation. She couldn't afford to let him under her radar. The more caring and concerned he was for her the more worried she was he might want to take something from her.

Ding-dong. Her doorbell didn't ring as often in a week as it had tonight.

'I'll get that. Take your time. There's plenty of hot water.' She closed the bathroom door before Conor said anything that could possibly change her mind and start to stir up her hormones. If he began peeling his clothes off in front of her, well… Risky, given how comfortable she was feeling with him. Almost as if she'd take a step off the edge to follow him. Almost. Went to show the state of her brain. Messy. Chaotic. In need of sleep.

'This green curry is delicious,' Tamara told Conor twenty minutes later as they lounged in her sitting room, laden plates on their knees. Hardly fine dining but very cosy. Her mother would have kittens if she saw her daughter like this in front of a man, especially as she was wearing a bathrobe that had seen better days a long time ago.

But you walked away from me, Mum, so your opinion doesn't count.

'I wasn't sure if you liked spicy food so I went with middling chilli.'

'It's yummy.' Her taste buds were in overdrive and even

her unreliable stomach was happy, though usually it was used to hot curry.

'Glad you like it.' Conor shuffled further back in the armchair he'd snagged earlier, pretending he wasn't yawning and all the while looking exhausted.

Then she thought of the cosy factor and the happiness retreated a step. Doing cosy with Conor when they had massive issues lying between them did not make sense. Even without the baby, cosy wasn't an option for her. Cosy would suck her in and leave her wide open for Conor to make everything go his way. At the moment she knew so little about him. Being sexually attracted to him didn't mean anything in this situation. She needed to get up to speed, and fast. Like checking the legal process for keeping her baby in New Zealand if he wanted to take it home to Ireland any time. Forewarned was forearmed. Protecting herself. Something she hadn't known to do with Peter. 'When you're not at work, what do you do with your time?'

His head tipped back and he blinked. Not expecting any questions? 'I run quite a lot, do the occasional half-marathon. Socialise, go fishing with Mac, visit places within easy driving distance.'

'Playing the tourist? I can't see you following the umbrella-waving guide and listening to a taped explanation about the geysers in Rotorua or the Hole in the Rock up north.'

His alluring mouth lifted in a wry smile. 'I am a visitor to this country. I might be working but I also want to see some of the sights. There's so much that's stunning. I could spend months just travelling the length and breadth of both islands.'

'Why do you want to go to Australia, then?' Or would that now be on hold?

Conor sat up straighter, stared at some place behind her.

'It's time to move on. Staying in one place too long often leads to complications.' Definitely holding back. 'Okay, make that it *was* time to move on. Everything's up in the air since your announcement. Apart from becoming a father.'

'You intend returning home some time?' Would he expect her to follow wherever he decided to go? Did she want to?

'Dublin is where I grew up, where all my family live. Dublin is who I am—what I am.' Was it her imagination or had his accent thickened?

'If that's how you feel, why leave in the first place?' What would it be like to live in Dublin? There was nothing to keep her in Auckland. On a positive note, there'd be no interfering television crews to bug her in Ireland.

He'd been yawning when she'd asked that question, but instantly his mouth slammed shut. The relaxed mood had gone in a blink.

When he didn't answer she gave him a break and changed the subject. 'Maybe you should stop running if it makes you so tired.'

'Never.' One word, spoken firmly, quietly, but full of *don't go there*.

It was all too much. They were going round in circles, and she didn't have the energy to try to figure it all out. Her eyes were itchy with tiredness, her head heavy and her body past ready for sleep. So she let it go. A voice in the back of her head was saying, *Look what happened last time you didn't ask the questions.* Not that she'd have got the right answers from Peter. Worry fired up. She bit down on it. Not tonight. 'You want a hot drink before you go home?'

He shook his head, the tightness in his shoulders easing again. 'You're right. I need to head away, give you some space. I've seen you're okay.' But he made no effort to move. 'It'll be time to get up and go to work soon enough.'

'Do you have to remind me?' Tamara hauled herself upright. 'I'm having some camomile tea.'

Conor's eyes locked on hers, causing her to hesitate.

Here we go. He's going to say something about the baby, and what we're going to do about it.

Her defences were rising and she made ready to protect herself.

'Thanks for this interlude.'

Thanks in full Irish lilt was not like thanks in Kiwi-speak. It came with warmth and intrigue and passion. It sent funny tingly sensations down her legs, along her arms. It said things she was certain Conor did not intend. And she had not expected. 'I didn't do anything.'

'Exactly. You could've started in on me about the baby, but instead you've been quiet and thoughtful.'

'I'm tired too.' Her breath stopped in her throat as she waited for the other shoe to fall.

'Exhaustion's puffing off you in clouds. It already was earlier in ED, which is why I had to make sure you'd got home safely and were looking after yourself.' Those lips twitched. 'After bad days at work I usually pace back and forth across my tiny apartment for hours on end. Tonight I don't feel wired, just shattered, yet okay with knowing I did everything I could for those kids, that I couldn't have done any more.'

'You're an amazing emergency specialist, always going the extra distance for your patients.'

Surprise lifted his thick eyebrows. 'But I never stop questioning myself, wondering what else I could've done. It's why I became an ED specialist in the first place. To save people.' Conor's hands tensed, his whole body winding tight. His mouth was flat as he dragged in air, then expelled it immediately. Those sunny summer eyes turned darker than an Auckland overcast day.

There was something else going on in his head that she had no line to.

Conor needed a hug.

Like that would solve anything. More likely he'd push her away. Wise man. Shoving her hands deep into the pockets of her robe, she turned for the kitchen and that tea, trying to ignore the painful squeeze her heart was giving.

They'd once shared a great night together that she'd enjoyed more than she'd have thought possible. Probably because she'd wanted nothing else from him than some fun. But that was it. End of. Except there was now a baby lying between them. There was no room for her heart to have its say.

Listening to her inner voice would undo all the effort she'd made over the last two years to get back on track. It'd also take more courage than she possessed, and would mean a breakdown of all the strictures she'd placed on herself to keep safe.

'Tamara.' Conor leaned against the doorjamb, watching her watch the kettle. He inhaled, sighed out the breath. 'Thanks. Again.'

'No problem.' Please go. Before she said something she regretted.

In a low, rolling version of that bone-melting accent Conor said, 'Don't be afraid to show me your true feelings or thoughts.'

Slowly turning, she stared at him, her heart now clunking heavily against her ribs. 'I'm not,' she muttered, and had to suffer the disbelief in his eyes. Fair cop. 'Okay, I've learned that showing my feelings about anything usually has severe repercussions.' When his mouth opened to spill words—a question?—she rushed in to cut him off. 'Not tonight.' Probably never. 'We're both in need of sleep, not long, convoluted conversations.'

Damn, but her head hurt. A steady throb pounded behind her eyes, matching her heart. There was only one cure. Bed. Alone. So she needed to drink her tea to help obtain that oblivion, and see Conor out the front door before hitting the sack. Not necessarily in that order either.

Why was the water taking for ever to boil?

Conor's eyelids were weighed down as he tried to open his eyes. 'Where the hell am I?'

He scoped the room, semi-lit from the hallway light, saw the cream leather armchairs and sighed. Tamara's place. Now he could feel that leather beneath his backside where he was sprawled along the matching couch. With a blanket covering him. When had Tamara put that there? Had to be her. There'd been no thought of him staying when they'd finished their meal and dumped the plates in the sink. No, he hadn't even done that much tidying up. She'd gone to make herself tea and he couldn't remember another thing after that. Except the ease with which he'd shifted from the chair to the couch and laid his head on a cushion.

The ease that had settled over him almost the moment he'd walked through Tamara's front door, despite his misgivings about coming here when they had a massive problem to deal with.

Careful. He'd be taking risks soon. Risks he'd spent the last fourteen years fighting. Risks that had had him finally fleeing Ireland and family and heart-aching despair. He couldn't imagine falling in love and getting married, having children. Children who might inherit his cardiac problem. A wife who could find herself bringing up their children alone because the big one had got him.

Conor sat up. Threw the blanket aside. Falling in love would mean breaking the rules that ran his life, kept everyone safe. So it wasn't happening.

A vision of Tamara looking gorgeous in her thick, faded navy-coloured robe with her dark blonde hair gone wild from her shower. Part of his brain had been functioning correctly when it had kept him from following through on the desire that had kicked up at the sight of her. It would've been the worst move possible, and there'd have been no thanks from Tam.

Don't call her that. The shortened version of Tamara disturbed her, for reasons he knew nothing about. And wanted to know. No, he mustn't. Knowing meant caring, meant sharing. But to him she was Tam. He just had to keep that to himself.

Time he was out of there. He needed to go home to his randomly put-together collection of furniture that was more practical than inviting; a home that spoke of moving on, not settling down.

Nothing like this warm and welcoming nest created with what he suspected were top-of-the-range furnishings. Not that he knew a lot about these things but this home seemed classy. That sideboard made of polished wood that he didn't recognise was stunning in its simplicity. In fact, everything was understated in a grand way. Was this why she didn't have a lot of spare money to go to university with? A shopaholic gone wild? If so, only when it came to her home. No money was wasted on clothes.

Who are you, Tamara Washington?

Deep down he knew he was never going to find out. His teeth ground as he leapt up to stretch the kinks from his body. He wanted to learn everything about her. Which would bring a load of problems best left well alone. It'd be easy to search on the web, but he didn't feel comfortable with that. That'd be a shallow act, and if Tamara couldn't find it in herself to tell him then best he left it alone.

A carved black clock with a gold face that had to be many decades old chimed once. Picking up his shoes, he made for the front door. Was Tamara all right? Sound asleep? Or was being overtired keeping her wide awake? He turned the other way.

At her bedroom door Conor stumbled. His lungs stalled and his heart slowed. Curled up on her side, her hands tucked under her chin, Tamara was sound asleep—and more beautiful than ever. Gone was that wariness with which she regarded the world, replaced with a gentleness and relief he'd not seen before. Relief because she was hiding from the world? Because she believed no one could get to her while she slept? Didn't she know she was at her most vulnerable when comatose?

His heart hammered in his chest. Excited or afraid? Didn't matter. He had to go home for what was left of the night. All it would take was to haul his tail down the hall and out the door to his car.

But he wasn't that strong. 'What's your history, Tam?' he whispered as he leaned down to lift an errant curl from her forehead. She approached people as though they were about to take something from her. Everyone except patients. They only needed what she was prepared to give.

As Conor reached to switch off the bedside lamp, she stirred. He held his breath, wishing her asleep. They both needed to get some hours' slumber before facing another day in the department.

Her eyes opened slowly. 'Conor?' His name slipped over her lips like melted chocolate, tantalising his taste buds and sending longing for more through his body, straight to his manhood.

'Yes, it's me,' he whispered. 'Go back to sleep.'

Before I can't control myself and haul you into my arms to kiss you senseless.

Because he wouldn't want to stop at kissing.

She snuggled her pillow around her neck. It was an innocent move and it stabbed him deeply.

And had him aiming for the front door.

Everything he'd been denying himself for many years was coming back to taunt him.

And those reasons weren't holding up as strongly as they usually did.

Get out of here. Fast.

CHAPTER FOUR

TAMARA WOKE SLOWLY, fighting her way through a haze. That had been the best sleep she'd had in weeks. No nightmares. No tears. Just plain old sleep.

Unwinding her body from its curled-up state, she pushed a foot across the bed, seeking Conor. Came up with empty space. Like why wouldn't she? Conor had not stayed the night.

For one, she hadn't wanted him to.

For two, he wouldn't have wanted to.

Three, she'd have been setting herself up for a crash.

Disappointment struck. She liked Conor Maguire. More than liked him. Charming, superb in bed, top-notch ED specialist, lots of fun at appropriate times. Hardly a résumé for the position of dad and partner in raising their child. But that shoe could fit her foot too. Her mother hadn't exactly set her up for this role.

So, like Conor or not, she had to keep him at a distance. At least until they'd had a serious talk about the baby. Several serious talks in which baby came first every time. Which meant keeping her heart uninvolved. Trusting that particular organ had once before led to monumental trouble with huge consequences affecting more people than herself. She would never subject her child to anything close to the destruction that falling in love with Peter had yielded.

'Your mummy's going to fight for everything you need, baby.' Her hands slid across her stomach, gently trying to feel the wee dot growing in there. As if. Hard to believe that something so small could create so much havoc.

Her stomach rolled uncomfortably. The first warning.

On the bedside table her phone rang. The screen read Conor. This early? Before work? Couldn't be good. 'Hello?'

'Just checking you were awake. Not sure if you set the alarm before you dropped into unconsciousness last night.' That Irishness surrounded her, warmed her, and tightened her stomach further.

'I didn't, but it seems I woke at my usual time anyway.' Her feet swung over the edge of the bed.

'You want me to pick you up this morning?'

That was getting too friendly. Her stomach lurched, another warning it wasn't going to play nice for much longer. 'I'll catch the bus as per normal. See you later.'

But he hadn't finished. 'Thought we could do breakfast at the Grafton Café, talk a bit about things so the day won't be too rocky, if you get my gist.'

No, no, no. Rolling her head from side to side, she dug deep to control her roiling stomach. 'I've got a couple of things to do before I leave for work.' Like throw up, for one. 'I'll see you there.'

'You can't avoid me, Tamara.' A thread of annoyance tightened that brogue.

'I'm not. It's just I don't do so well with breakfast at the moment. See you at work.' Got to run. 'Bye.' She threw herself out of bed and down the short hall to the bathroom. That had been far too close.

Tamara rushed into the department a little before seven thirty, knowing she looked dishevelled. 'Sorry I'm late,' she gasped as she struggled to get her breath back after running from the bus stop.

'Where have you been?' Conor asked. 'I was getting worried.'

'You don't need to keep track of me all the time because of—' *Quiet*. Lots of ears around here. 'I got busy with things and lost track of time.'

'You're never late.' A furrow formed between his eyes. 'You've been crying.'

Not *crying* crying. 'Soap in my eyes.' Her life had done an abrupt turn. Of course there'd be the occasional tear.

Conor's delectable lips didn't look so tempting when they pressed together tightly. Neither were his eyes the light, sparkling blue of a kingfisher any more. He ground out, 'Try again.'

The ambulance bay buzzer saved her from answering. 'I'll get that.' She raced away before someone else could take the case and leave her to deal with Conor's questions.

'Morning.' Kelli bounced alongside her. 'Did I sleep well last night, or what? The only good thing to come out of that bus accident.'

'I had the best sleep in for ever,' Tamara agreed. Not that she'd felt that flash since baby had had its say first thing.

'Conor's got a glare going on this morning.' Kelli nodded back at the department hub. 'Any idea what's brought that on?'

Tamara blanched, and tripped over her own feet. 'Why ask me?'

'Just wondering if something's going on between the two of you.'

'You've got an overactive imagination, Kelli Watts.'

'You're overreacting to a simple statement, Tamara Washington.' Kelli grinned. 'The man's hot, and you're single.'

'I'm still getting over my last mistake,' Tamara snapped.

Kelli's hands went up in submission. 'I'm sorry for teasing you, but sometimes you need to let go of the past enough to have some fun at least. Who better to get back in the saddle with than a gorgeous Irish doctor who's not hanging around for ever?'

Couldn't argue with that. So she didn't. But Kelli still had to be shut down in a hurry. Just knowing all about what had gone down with Peter didn't give her the right to interfere. 'The thing is, I don't want to get back in the saddle. That leads to complications and I've had my share of those.'

And I have another, bigger one under my waistband right now.

'You know what, girlfriend? Not all men are devious, manipulative, nasty pieces of work like your ex.' Kelli's words were followed with a quick hug.

'Yet you avoid Mac like the plague.' Tamara was certain her friend was halfway to being in love with the night-shift specialist.

'Low blow.' Kelli stepped back. 'But you're forgiven since you are very wrong.'

They reached the ambulance line. 'Who's this?' Tamara asked the ambulance officer standing with the stretcher.

'Cassandra Wright, thirty-three. The car she was a passenger in was involved in a nose-to-tail car accident on the southern motorway,' they were told. 'The driver's in a second ambulance about to arrive.'

'Hello, Cassandra. I'm Tamara, and this is Kelli. We're nurses. I hear you had an argument with the windscreen.'

The woman was wearing a neck brace, and blood covered most of her face from abrasions to her forehead and chin. 'Stupid of me not to put my seat belt on.'

Definitely. 'We'll take you through to ED so one of the

doctors can examine you,' Tamara told her. 'Have you got a headache?'

'A blinder,' Cassandra acknowledged.

'Any numbness, pins and needles?'

'No.' She shook her head, then winced. 'Ouch. I can turn my head either way. That's got to be good.'

'We'll be cautious until the doctor's seen you.' The neck brace was standard with any head injuries, and hopefully it wouldn't be needed for much longer.

In a cubicle it was all hands to the blanket as they transferred Cassandra onto a bed. Then Tamara began attaching leads from the heart monitor to the pads already stuck on the woman's chest. 'We're off to a busy start.' At least that'd keep Conor from slipping under her skin and turning her into a nervous wreck.

'Welcome to the A team, Cassandra.' Conor strode in, taking up space and air in the cubicle. 'After yesterday we can handle anything,' he said in a quiet aside to Tamara and Kelli.

The buzzer went again. 'That'll be Cassandra's friend,' Tamara muttered. 'I'll bring her in.' Kelli could work with Conor and she'd go with another doctor. Fingers crossed. She needed distance from Conor while coming to terms with his new role in her life.

Tamara reached her next patient, grateful for the distraction. She was told, 'Suspected concussion, fractured left wrist, and upper arm pain where she hit the steering wheel. Obs are good.'

From then on they were busy, but after yesterday no one was complaining about the steady stream of patients with mid-level urgency.

At five past ten Tamara looked up from typing obs into a patient's file on the computer and said to Kelli, 'Take a break while you can.' Having got over its morning petulance, her stomach was rumbling with hunger.

Conor leaned over the counter. 'I shouted Danish pastries for everyone. After yesterday we deserve a treat.'

'I'm out of here.' Kelli grinned and headed away as the desk phone rang.

'That's good of you,' Tamara sighed as her stomach sat up to attention. 'I love Danish pastries.'

'I've noticed.' Conor dropped some ambulance patient notes into the 'finished' basket.

He hadn't bought them especially for her, had he? She studied him and got a shrug in return. 'Thanks. I —' The phone continued ringing. 'I'll be there in a minute.' Hopefully.

The first tummy-tightening smile of the day appeared. 'I'll save you two.'

By the time Tamara had dealt with the haematology tech about a CBC result the department was quiet. As was the crammed kitchen space when she walked in.

'Tamara.' Kelli was at her side, her voice troubled.

'What?' Her antenna was up and rotating as she looked around at the faces of her colleagues watching her.

'Same old, same old,' one of them muttered, and drank from her mug.

'What's happened?'

Conor stepped in front of her and reached for her elbow. 'Bring your coffee to my office.'

Her stomach dived, right to the floor. The idea of food was suddenly abhorrent. When Conor tugged her gently she stood strong, kept both feet planted firmly on the floor. 'Tell me.' Why did this sensation swamping her feel so familiar? She dropped her gaze to the table.

Newspaper headlines screamed out at her.

Heiress Making Good for Her Misdemeanours?

Beneath that was a colour photo of Tamara and Conor in Resus One, working on their wee patient's foot—or where his foot had once been.

Nurse Tamara Washington and Dr Conor Maguire in the emergency department, working to save the children involved in yesterday's horrendous bus accident on the motorway.

'Will this never go away? Why won't they let me get on with my life?' She slapped her hands on her hips in an attempt to stop the shaking. 'Then again, why am I even surprised? They're never going to let me live my pathetic little life in peace.' Of course the media weren't going to drop anything about the rich young woman who'd tantalised them for years and now sold papers and turned on TVs just by living. Every time this happened it was another slap across her face, saying *See, this is what happens when you get involved with wicked men.*

'Breathe, Tam.' Conor spoke quietly beside her.

She hadn't been aware she'd stopped. Apparently her lungs had given up the ghost. If only her brain could follow. At least until her rage died down to a disgruntled angst. About the middle of next year.

Angry tears slid down her face. Frustration made her clench her hands so her fingers were bruising her hips. 'I hope something's been done to beef up security. No reporters should've got in here.'

Conor nodded. 'I've talked to the CEO. It won't happen again.'

'Hope he realises they're persistent by nature.'

'You know all about that?' Conor asked. He knew little

or nothing about her past, and she'd liked it that way. Could be why she'd allowed herself to get closer to him than she did anyone else. Except Kelli, but she'd been there for her the whole way through.

'Sit down before you fall down.' Conor pulled a chair from the table and took her elbow to direct her.

One step and that blasted newspaper got all her attention. Her hands were shaking so badly she couldn't pick it up so she pressed them to the table, either side of the evil missive, and stared at the words.

'Don't read it, Tamara. You know what they're saying. It's old hat.' Kelli made to remove the paper.

Tamara slapped one hand bang in the centre, anchoring the paper on the table. Old habits forced her to read everything the media wrote or said about her. A tear splashed onto the newsprint.

'Here.' Conor passed over a handful of tissues before putting his hand back on her shoulder, his thumb immediately going into soothing mode by rubbing circles over her. He must've read this and now had more knowledge than she cared for.

'Guess you had to find out sometime,' she snapped. Longing for normal hit her. The need to lean back against Conor without having to consider the ramifications was very strong. But history kept her still. She'd be fooling herself. Nothing was right, and didn't look like becoming so in the near future. Whenever a reporter wrote yet another sensational article about her she folded, let them walk all over her with their comments. Some were kind, but no better with their fawning comments about the girl who'd been sucked in by the fraudulent lawyer than those who said she was as guilty for making it easy for Peter to get away with her father's fortune, and hurting others along the way. She slashed at her wet cheeks with the tissues.

You have a baby growing inside you.

The truth sideswiped her, shoved everything else to the back of her skull, settled the turmoil back into the smouldering anger which she drew on to redirect her thoughts.

She had to toughen up. This was no longer just about her. These people mustn't be allowed to hurt her any more, because they'd be affecting her child.

Glancing around, she saw only Conor and Kelli left in the room. The low murmurings outside the door indicated everyone else must've stepped outside the kitchenette to give her space. At least they knew the score. 'I presume someone's already filled you in on my past.' She nodded at her baby's father.

'Not at all, and if this morning's reaction is anything to go by I don't think anyone's bothered except for how it affects you.' His fingers were gentle on her shoulder. 'The media can't destroy you if you don't let them, Tam.'

She jerked sideways, away from that warmth. 'Don't call me Tam.' Now the tears were a flood. 'Dad called me that. My wonderful dad.' She stabbed the headline glaring up at her. 'I let him down so badly that I don't deserve to be called Tam.'

'That's a lie,' Kelli growled. 'You weren't the first person Peter ripped off, and I bet when he gets out of jail, you won't be the last. He fooled your father first, remember?'

Tamara gasped. 'Kelli.' Where had her supportive friend gone?

'It's true, and it's about time you acknowledged that instead of taking all the blame. As in really accepted it deep down. Conor's right. Stop letting these guys hurt you.' The words were harsh but Kelli's smile was kind. 'Only thinking of you, girlfriend.' That knowing glint from earlier was back in her eyes as she glanced at Conor. 'I'll go and cover for you while you get your mojo back.'

If only it was that simple. But, yes, she could no longer sit around sulking, or dreaming up ways to kill off every reporter walking the country. 'Thanks, Kells.' Then she turned to the man who deserved an explanation. He hadn't disappeared out the door; neither did he look starved for the gossip. He only appeared concerned—for her.

'Have you read any of that?' Tamara nodded at the article.

'Didn't finish the first paragraph. I can't stand idle nastiness. You're not that person he's written about, Tamara. Nor has anyone around here told me anything. I suppose they all think it old hat and don't need to bring me up to speed. If I'm going to learn what it's all about I'd prefer you told me.'

'You don't think I'll paint a dishonest picture about being the victim to keep you onside?'

'No.'

'You have no idea, and yet...' He didn't understand the gift he'd given her. Warmth swamped her, right down to her toes.

Conor was spooning coffee into a fresh mug, and now he hesitated. Turning to look her in the eye, he seemed to be searching for something. And she really needed him to find it. Whatever it was. They had a baby to think about. Even her own future was waving at her. The next few minutes were going to have a lasting effect on how that went once Conor knew about her past mistakes.

Sinking onto a chair, she turned the paper over. As Conor had said, she could tell the story without the innuendo and nastiness. Propping her elbows on the table and her chin in her hands, she began. 'I grew up in a wealthy family. Dad started an engineering company when he was twenty-one, and went from strength to strength, making a fortune. Timing was everything, and he'd hit it bang on.

I had the life of a princess, and I certainly took on that role very well.'

Conor placed a mug in front of her. 'Get some of that in you.'

Liquid didn't slop on the table when she picked it up. It had to be Conor's calming influence because her body wasn't feeling completely out of kilter as normally happened when she talked about her beloved father. 'Dad wanted me to join the company but I was determined to become a nurse. If I hadn't been in such a hurry to prove I could do anything I chose, I might've figured out that I really wanted to study medicine and become a doctor.' But that was another story, and irrelevant. She was avoiding the real screw-up in the room. A mouthful of coffee and she put the mug down. 'Peter Gillespie was the company lawyer, a hotshot man who charmed everyone. Including me. I fell hook, line and sinker. We got engaged, but the wedding kept being postponed for one reason or another. Mum wasn't happy with the venue or Peter wanted to invite someone who wouldn't be able to attend on that date. Then Dad was diagnosed with dementia.'

More tissues appeared in her line of vision. 'Take it slowly.'

'I haven't talked about this for so long I should be rusty, but the words are always there, banked up in the back of my skull ready to spill any time I press the button.'

'How old were you when you got engaged?'

'Twenty-three. Old enough to know better.' Her sigh was bitter. 'But, then, I was used to people falling into line with me. Peter seemed to be following the same path. He was a lot older than I was. I liked that.' His age had lent itself to his authenticity. Yep, she'd been naïve.

Conor sat opposite her, not staring at her as though she

was a nutcase, or avidly hanging onto every word and waiting for the dirty details.

If she wanted to fall in love, here was the perfect man. But she didn't, so no go. 'I was twenty-five when Dad's dementia became apparent, and a year later he was beyond running his company.'

'Fast, then. Or had he been hiding it?'

'A bit of both, not that anyone can conceal having dementia. But he was clever at covering his errors until— until he couldn't any more.' She scratched at a mark on the table as some of the heartbreaking memories rose before her. 'Fast was best. I'd have hated for him to take years of slowly diminishing before us. Watching him was hard enough anyway.'

Conor's hand covered hers, gentle and caring. There was no need for words. He understood her pain.

But would he understand the worst? Pulling her hand free, she leaned back to put space between them. Being strong, right? 'I, along with the lawyer and head accountant, had been given power of attorney over Dad's companies and personal assets.'

See where I'm going with this?

'I gave up my hospital job to nurse Dad, and when that became too much we brought in other nurses to help me. The mental aspects of looking after him were appalling, but seeing my once fit and active father turn into a small, wizened man was equally heartbreaking.'

'You were distraught, unable to cope with anything else.' The guy got it on every level. Scary. Didn't mean she could trust him yet.

'Peter seized his opportunity. He already oversaw all business decisions, but he kindly read documents and affirmed their content so I only had to sign them. He invested company money, made policy decisions. All to give me more time with Dad, you understand. The accountant wasn't any less helpful either. Between them they were well qualified to run the business, whereas I was too easy to fool.' She held the mug, rolled it back and forth in her hands, staring into the murky brown liquid like she might finally find some answers in there, yet knew she was deceiving herself. 'I let them steal everything from us. I let them.'

'It must've been difficult, dealing with your dad's situation and keeping tabs on a huge business, which, as you said yourself, you weren't qualified to do. Did you have grounds to doubt Peter's loyalty to your father? To you?'

'None. No one did. He was always so willing to help, to be there whenever Dad asked for him, even when Dad couldn't remember who he was half the time. Right up until the end, Peter would turn up every morning to have the business meeting they'd spent years having, despite Dad not comprehending a word.'

'How did you find out what he'd done?' Still nothing but concern and care radiated out at her from across the table. Scary or compelling?

Tamara dropped her gaze from Conor, afraid of the hope he'd started waking up inside her. Instead, she stared at the tabletop, focusing on that awful day that had culminated in ruin, seeing everything, including Peter's smug face, as clearly as if it had happened yesterday, today even. How had she been so stupid not to see what he was doing? How?

'Tam?'

'Don't,' she whispered.

'You're Tam to me, and nothing you've told me will change that.'

Hadn't he heard everything she'd said? Or not understood it fully? Finish the story, get back to work. Work where all her colleagues would be watching her, even when it was old news to most of them. An ache encompassed her. She'd had enough of that, didn't want another round of feeling like a fruit loop. 'We'd been home from Dad's funeral less than an hour when the fraud squad arrived and all hell broke loose.' Flashing cameras, shouted questions, pushy reporters trying to get in her face.

'The media had a field day, huh?' His expression still hadn't changed.

Maybe she did have another friend in this world. 'They'd been at the funeral, and followed the procession to the cemetery, then on to our home afterwards. All my supposed friends had plenty to gossip about, and appeared to be very knowledgeable on things they couldn't have had a clue about. Even my mother talked about me.' Her voice faded away to a strangled whisper. 'I was to blame, you see. I let Peter sign the papers that shifted funds offshore into bank accounts that did not have Washington Enterprises in their name.'

'Your mother didn't have signing rights?' Conor asked.

'Now, there's the irony. Dad knew she'd be forever signing papers without a clue what they were about. As long as there was enough money in her accounts to keep up with the lifestyle she adored then everything was fine in her world. Besides...' She hesitated, suddenly feeling disloyal to her mother, a woman who'd not often shown her any loyalty most of her life. But Conor needed to know who he was getting involved with for his child's sake. 'Mum is a bit of a loose cannon, never stops to think of the consequences of anything she wants to do.'

'Where is she now?'

'Living with a distant relative in a small town in Australia.'

Conor rose and came around to her, held out his hands to haul her to her feet. His hug was gentle and reassuring. He wasn't about to trash her for her past. If only she could truly trust him she might risk falling under his spell. Might. But, no, there was too much at stake. They hadn't even begun sorting out the future for their child.

'You want to take the rest of the day off?' he asked, still holding her close.

Yes. Home seemed like the perfect place to be right now. Close the curtains, turn on the TV, though not the news channel, and pull a blanket up to her ears. But she'd done that too often. Straightening out of his arms, she eyeballed him. 'I'm not leaving before the end of the shift.'

'Go, you.' His smile pinged her right in the tummy. 'I've got your back all the way.'

Unease slipped in. 'Why, Conor?'

He looked taken aback at the question. He was certainly thinking about it. 'I just do, that's why.'

She nodded. The best answer in the world. He was accepting her for who she was, despite not knowing her too well. When was the last time that had happened? Yet she still didn't fully trust him. Because of Peter.

Another reason could be that her world was righting itself. Then her stomach cramped, reminding her of the baby. She was fooling herself. And Conor.

CHAPTER FIVE

'TOO MANY PATIENTS for a Tuesday afternoon,' Conor muttered under his breath as yet another yawn pulled out of him. 'Tuesdays are meant to be slow. Tuesdays following the Monday we had yesterday at any rate.'

A woman burst into the cubicle. 'Mum, what happened? I told you to come and live with us but, no, you want to be independent and this is what happens.' She bent down to plant a loud kiss on his patient's cheek.

'Hello, dear. I had a fall, that's all. It would've happened wherever I was.' Mrs Gowan was beaming at her daughter.

'Yes, but then I'd have been able to help you.' The daughter tugged a chair up to the bed and reached for her mother's hand.

Tamara was watching them with something like envy in her expression. Something else in her background he had yet to learn about. She'd said her mother had dumped on her with the media, but why?

Another yawn ripped out of him. Damn, he hadn't been this tired since he'd been in nappies. A red flag went up. He hadn't been like this for fourteen years. Since his heart attack.

Shock rocked him back on his heels. Was this a precursor to another cardiac incident? His head spun. No way.

'All normal there.' On the other side of the bed Tamara unwrapped the BP cuff from Meredith Gowan's arm.

After that jolt over the newspaper article Tamara was coping well. He'd kept her at his side, brought her into all his cases, stared down any staff member who gave her a questioning look. Not that many had. It seemed most of them knew the story and didn't need to rehash the details.

'Dr Maguire.' Tamara spoke firmly. 'Mrs Gowan?' She nodded at their patient. Definitely not one for schmoozing over him despite that hot night they'd had in bed. Instead, she kept him on his toes, and for some perverse reason that made him worry he might fail her. He was good at looking out for people, just as long as he didn't get involved.

Ah, hello? You're having a baby together. Whether you want to or not. Is that not involvement?

A sudden, clenching ache gripped him in the chest. Panic unfurled, ramped through him, sending fingers of shock expanding throughout his chest, his gut.

Tamara appeared in front of him. 'Are you all right? Should I get Michael to take over here?' Her voice was filled with nothing but concern. For him.

'I'm fine.' His chest tightened further.

I am not having a heart attack. I know what that feels like and it's not this.

Nodding abruptly at Tamara, he dropped his gaze to his patient. Away from those all-seeing eyes still focused on him. 'This fall you had today? Run through what happened. I know you've told the triage nurse but I'd like to hear it myself.' Mrs Gowan might add something previously overlooked. Concentrating hard on the answers could keep the growing tightness in his chest at bay, help him calm down.

'I was coming down the steps from the laundry to the

porch and next thing I know I'm on my back, staring up at the sky, Doc.'

'Did you trip over something? Slip on the step?' The pain was not abating.

'I don't remember anything like that. One minute I was upright, the next I wasn't.'

At least Mrs Gowan had been conscious when it had happened to her. 'Can you recall any dizziness?' Conor asked as he rubbed his temples. Talk about feeling off balance. And he was the doctor. Leaning his thigh against the bed, he blindly studied the page in his hand while listening to his patient with all the attentiveness he could muster.

'Conor?' Tamara remained near him, that concern now reflected in her eyes.

He flicked his gaze in her direction for a quick fix to hang onto and clashed with a serious enquiry on Tamara's face.

'I'm getting Michael.'

Not what Conor wanted to hear. 'Stay with your patient.' His chest wall gave a squeeze, reminding him of what he was trying to ignore. *Think like a doctor, man.* Not a useless twit who panics at the slightest twinge. Get someone, Tamara, to check his pulse, put him on the monitor for a heart reading. But then everyone would know his dirty little secret.

The air whipped around Tamara as she stomped to the head of the bed.

I'm light-headed and my chest's tight, the panic's rising, but otherwise I'm good to go.

'Mrs Gowan…' He tapped her notes. 'This says you haven't had any headaches recently, no unusual chest discomfort.'

'Nothing, Doc.'

Tamara had some serious questions for him. He knew

how her gaze could shine with wicked delight and hot anticipation, and how the brown shade could sparkle like hot chocolate. He'd seen fun and laughter twinkle in Tamara's eyes for the first time that night two months ago. He'd also seen despair and sadness dull them at work when she thought no one was watching. There were many layers to this woman. Layers he wanted to probe and learn about, to peel back and reveal her depths. Now she was watching him like a hungry falcon.

Crack. His chest tightened. While his head lightened. He did not want Tamara knowing about this. She'd draw him in, get too close, want to fix him. They were going to be parents together. He couldn't. Not when at any moment a heart attack might take him out of the picture, like it had Dad and his brother.

'Are we transferring Mrs Gowan to the medical ward?' Tamara knew damned well they weren't until they had some answers to what'd happened to her. She was hitting him over the head with a sharp reminder to focus on his work. Strange how quickly things turned around. A short time ago he'd been helping her to pull herself together.

Conor swayed on his feet and fought the need to reach out for the bed to steady himself. He also ignored the way Tamara looked at him. Like he shouldn't be here. 'Right. I'll arrange some blood tests before we go any further.' He disappeared through the curtains without another word. Not the usual friendly, 'take as long as you want' Dr Maguire, but 'I need to sit down before I fall down' Dr Maguire.

He diverted directly into the next cubicle and stopped by the bed.

My chest's too tight.

Those old memories of chest pain crashed through his mind.

My breathing's all over the place.

He knew how to calm down by drawing long, slow breaths into his lungs, huffing them straight back out. Knew the muscles holding his chest would eventually let go their fierce grip.

I am not having a heart attack.

This was a panic attack. Simple as that. He knew those. Hadn't had one for over a year. The tightness in his chest muscles wasn't easing off. What if he was wrong? What if he deserted his child before it made its appearance?

'Conor?' Tamara stood in front of him, reaching for his arms. 'Tell me what's going on,' she demanded.

Lifting his head far too fast, he growled, 'Can't a man have a moment to himself around here?' He should've taken his time straightening up before answering her. Should've. Didn't. Swaying, he grabbed for something to hold onto. Unfortunately, Tamara was the first stable thing within reach. Thing? Sorry. Nothing *thing*-like about her with all those curves she kept hidden under layers of baggy clothes.

'Sit down.' She tried to shove him onto the bed.

He pushed her hands away. 'I'm fine,' he ground out through a wave of panic. Not pain.

'And I'm a monkey's backside.' She did those retorts so well. They could burn a man if he wasn't careful.

'I can honestly say I don't agree with you about that.' Focusing on annoying Tamara might help distract from the panic building relentlessly.

Her mouth flattened into a warning.

Quick, defuse her. 'I'm overtired.'

'So you said.' Her brows came together into a danger-ous frown. 'I'm not buying it.'

Faster, man. Or next she'll have the whole crew in here. 'I ran in the Auckland marathon on Saturday.' The frown didn't soften. She was seeing right through his attempts to divert her, something she was obviously better at than him. 'Throw in that busload of broken children and your news, it's hardly surprising I'm a bit wobbly on my feet.'

At last. No more frown. Instead, those luscious lips that had once played havoc on his feverish skin were tight and uncompromising, while hurt stabbed at him from those eyes he couldn't forget. Hurt and...? Disappointment. No, distrust. Like he'd let her down big time. Over what? Try not being honest with her. Right, like he'd tell her about his family history of cardiac problems right here, now. Going to have to sometime, though. That baby might already be in trouble.

'Right.' She snatched the patient notes out of his hand. 'What blood tests did you want done on Mrs Gowan?'

'CBC, electrolytes, LFTs. And a CRP.'

'Right,' she repeated, and stalked off, those shoulders almost meeting in the middle of her back and her chin shoved forward.

He could've added how he hadn't slept much in weeks for thinking about her and that amazing body she never showcased in fitted clothes.

What was with her frumpy style of dress anyway? Surely that had nothing to do with what her ex had done? Most females would kill for a figure like Tamara's. He hadn't expected it and could still feel the wonder he'd known as he'd undressed her before caressing her from top to toe. And back again. It had been like unwrapping a gift he had asked for and finding something far more exciting. That, and how she'd reacted with blatant enjoyment to his lovemaking.

Sex. He did not make love. He had sex with willing women and said goodbye in the morning. No fault with that. He was saving a potential partner and any children they might have from a life-load of worry and fear.

Got that wrong, hadn't he?

Slam. The clouds in Conor's skull thickened, his muscles tightened. Breathe in, out. In, out. Still no pain. Not a heart attack. Relief flooded his tense body to loosen the tautness, push the fog in his head aside. Thank goodness for something. Stretching his arms high, he rolled his head in a circle to loosen the tension in his neck until finally he felt capable of functioning as a doctor again.

Blasted panic attacks. No accounting for when they made an appearance.

'You all right?' Kelli asked when he returned to the counter, where Tamara was fiercely intent on entering details in a patient's file on the computer.

'Absolutely.' A quick glance at the wall clock. Thirty minutes to go and he'd be out of there. Straight home, no stopping at the supermarket for food that would sit in the fridge until he threw it out next week. No, he'd put his feet up, chuck on a CD and order in something to eat. Probably fall asleep and wake up in the morning all stiff and achy. But at least his heart would be ticking along perfectly. The last traces of that panic that'd been overwhelming him had evaporated.

Twenty-nine minutes to go.

You and Tamara need to talk.

Double damn.

Conor snatched up the top file of waiting patients and stalked off to the waiting room. 'Jason Grove?'

Twenty-eight minutes to go.

Tamara pressed 'talk' on her phone and held it to her ear.

'Hello?' came the voice she'd known all her life.

Surprising how her mother hadn't put her name in her phone by now just so as she didn't have to answer her calls. 'Hi, Mum. Don't hang up. Please. I've got something—'

Click. 'Important to tell you.' She stared at the far wall of her lounge. No surprise there. Shouldn't have bothered trying. But seeing Mrs Gowan so happy when her daughter had raced into ED that afternoon, she'd wanted to talk to her own mother right there and then. Wanted to connect, to share about the baby, to be a family again.

Tamara slammed the phone onto the armrest of the recliner and stared off into nowhere. Her favourite place when everything was going pear-shaped.

Please, talk to me one day, Mum. I want to hear you say my name again. Could even do with one of your whacky hugs right about now. I know I screwed up but I don't think all the blame was mine.

Huh? That was new. Of course it had been her fault. She'd been the one to trust Peter. Not the only one, as Kelli had pointed out. Dad had too, long before her.

Conor hadn't freaked out or blamed her. He'd listened to her story and carried on like she wasn't a complete waste of space. Was that why she'd tried to contact her mum tonight? Because he'd stirred up some hope inside her? Dangerous stuff. Especially when it came to her mother.

Ding-dong. That blasted doorbell sure was getting a workout this week. Tamara chose to ignore it. Note to self: take batteries out when whoever was out there had gone.

She could understand Conor's exhaustion. If indeed that was all that had tipped him off his feet earlier—and the jury was still out on that. Fatigue dripped off her, leaving her body barely able to drag itself around the flat. There was no energy left in the tank to entertain a visitor.

If Kelli had come bearing wine and food for a girls' night of chatting then sorry, but she wasn't coming in. Tamara huffed a sigh. Drinking was out these days with a baby under her belt. Not that she'd ever indulged much.

Ding-dong.

If it was Conor then tonight she wasn't able to face him and the endless questions he'd have about where she was with planning the future for her and baby. Especially when he hadn't been forthcoming about that episode in ED knocking him sideways. They both had to be upfront, not just her. Hell, Conor had spent the remainder of the shift barking at just about everyone who moved, while sending her strange looks that had explained absolutely nothing. And reminded her not to trust him too quickly.

Ding-dong.

'Go away.'

Her phone pinged. Conor.

I know you're in there, Tamara.

Ding-dong.

The door hit the wall when she tugged it open. 'Not tonight, Conor. You had your space, now I want mine.'

The guy just walked on in, like he hadn't heard a word she'd said. 'Not happening.'

Guess he had heard then. 'Excuse me? You think you can walk all over me as you choose?' Like Peter had. She growled, 'Don't walk away like that.' The words were strong but her voice lacked real grit. Damn, this toughening up wasn't as easy as she'd hoped.

Conor spun back to face her, hands on hips like earlier in the day. 'I am not walking all over you. What I am doing is making certain you understand I will be a part of this, that I will always support you. I will not be shoved away.'

'I don't remember shoving you anywhere.' She *had* tried to push him onto the bed when he'd been having his moment in ED.

'Just so you're fully aware. After what you told me today about your ex I want you to know I stand at your side.'

She'd take her time over that, assimilate more about him and how he reacted to situations and other people. 'Right. Message received loud and clear. Now can you go?'

'We have things to discuss, and I for one do not believe in putting them off.'

'Oh, really?'

Conor swallowed hard. 'Yes, really. Delay only leads to worry and more problems.' He stared at her, as though waiting for her to fold. 'We already left talking about the baby last night.'

He had a valid point. Unfortunately. But she wasn't folding. Shoving her chin out, Tamara said, 'Fair enough. But be warned, I'm shattered and will kick you out the moment I need to go to bed.' Like about now. Oh, and make that go to bed *alone*. Two in her bed would require energy and trust and knowing where they were headed with baby. Which led right back to what Conor had said as he'd walked in.

'I hear you. Not everything is going to go my way.'

'You're onto it.' This new her, the stronger version, the less trusting type, seemed to be working. Amazing what pregnancy did to a girl. If she had to be a mother, then she'd give it her all to be the best.

Closing the door, she headed for the lounge and the big recliner to curl up in. Comfortable was the only way to go.

She didn't make it that far. As she stepped past him Conor caught her hands gently, shook her softly. 'Look at me, Tamara.'

Then she'd be lost. He'd be able to demand anything.

No, he wouldn't. Less trusting until you know more about him, remember? Charm doesn't cut it when dealing with major decisions.

The gaze she met was serious, with tenderness hovering at the edges. Her mouth dried. Why hadn't she met Conor before Peter? Her life might've been so different. Now all she could do was put her baby first. 'Yes?'

'How are you keeping? You hinted at morning sickness when I phoned early. Other physical discomforts?'

Knock me down with a feather.

He was doing *nice* to perfection. A ruse? She stared at him, delved into that gaze, searched for lies. Got only honesty. She didn't think she was wrong. Not with Conor. Or was that more wishful thinking on her part? She'd go with it for now, see where it led. 'Like I said, I don't do breakfast any more. It has a habit of regurgitating.'

'Hence those big morning teas you've started indulging in this week.'

Tamara nodded. 'I get a bit tired. Otherwise all's good.' She made to pull her hands free. His hold was compelling and she didn't want to throw herself at him, needed space between them.

Conor had other ideas. His hands tightened around hers. 'You won't have been to a midwife or your GP yet.'

'Give me time. I've only known since Friday and the first hurdle was to let you know.'

'Hurdle?' Hurt crossed his eyes. 'I'm an obstacle in all of this?' Now her hands were free, dropped like hot coals as he stepped back from her.

'Wrong choice of word.' When he continued to stare at her, she hurried to explain, though not a hundred percent sure what her problem was. There were too many of them. Sigh. 'I'm getting my head around the fact I'm pregnant. I still have no clue what you're thinking about becoming a parent.'

'Not good enough, Tamara. It was always going to be a shock for me, which I'm supposing it was for you, but you're coming through it, as I will.'

She moved past him, dropped into her chair. 'I'm going

to be completely honest, though you might not like what I say.'

'Can it be any worse than what you've already hit me with?' He took the chair opposite but didn't relax back into it, sat instead with his elbows on his knees, his chin in his hands.

'Any worse? I get that an unplanned pregnancy is the last thing most of us want, but it's not the end of the world,' she snapped. 'I want this baby now that I have it growing inside me.'

It was true. *It was true.* Her hand spread across her stomach. She hadn't allowed herself to believe that one day she'd be a parent, yet it was happening. *Oh, my.*

'I'm going to do everything possible to look out for this baby.'

'You're days ahead of me, but I do not want to get rid of it, if that's what you were implying.'

So much for thinking they were starting to get along quite well. They didn't understand each other at all. 'I wasn't.' Silence crept into the room as she strung her thoughts into a cohesive statement. She had one shot at explaining herself. Finally, 'I told you about my past and what Peter did. What I didn't go into was the screw-up I became afterwards, and mostly still am. I used to trust everyone, now I trust no one. Hence all that dithering about my med school application.' She locked her eyes on his. 'Do I trust you to do the right thing by our child? Absolutely.' She paused, swallowed hard.

Damn you, Peter. You ruined everything for me. But, then, you wouldn't give a toss, would you?

'I hear a "but"…'

Again silence reigned. Until she gathered up her courage and told him the truth. 'I am afraid of what you might want to do regarding our child. Will you try to take him from me? Go back to Ireland with him? I'm going with calling the baby him for now as I hate saying it.'

Conor's face was tightening, his eyes darkening dangerously, but he refrained from uttering a word.

So she continued, digging a bigger hole. 'Do I trust you to do the right thing by me? I…' Swallowing the bile building up in her mouth, she tried again. 'Honestly? I want to. I want to believe *in* you, but I don't believe in my judgement.' She sank back, huddled in on herself, becoming small and tense. No sign of her new, stronger backbone, but, then, she had managed to put the truth out there so she had to get points for that. Didn't she?

'Firstly, I will never take the baby away from you.' Conor ground out the words through clenched teeth. 'Just so you know,' he added with as much anger as she'd ever seen in him.

'Thank you.' Did she trust him on that score? Yes, she thought she did. 'I didn't really think you would, but as I said I have trouble believing everything first time up.'

Any relief was short-lived. 'Whether I return to Ireland with my child—and you—is something I cannot say yet. But you should know I've always intended returning home at some stage. For good.'

'Is that non-negotiable?'

Conor nodded. 'I thought it was. But that was before the baby announcement. Of course it'd now be up for discussion.' He paused. 'Could you ever consider moving to Ireland?'

'Since I've been intent on hiding away these past two years I hadn't thought about moving anywhere, but I'll put Ireland on the list of changes to be contemplated.' Why not up sticks and head to the northern hemisphere? As Kelli had pointed out, she had nothing to stay here for. Even better, no one in Ireland would know her history, would chase her with cameras or ask for comments on everything from fraud to investment funds. A move out of New Zealand could work in her favour. 'You never fully explained what brought you Down Under.'

'I wanted a change.'

'From what?'

'My family.' What wasn't he telling her?

'Thought you adored them.'

Conor leapt to his feet, stared around the lounge and sank back down. 'I do. All of them. But it's like happy families, all my sisters married and producing delightful little offspring. I was overwhelmed.'

'You're not telling me everything.' See? Knew not to trust him completely.

'Whether I return home or decide to stay in New Zealand or move to Australia, I won't shirk my responsibilities, Tamara.' A non-answer if ever she'd heard one.

It didn't bode well for trusting him completely. 'Being a parent isn't all about responsibilities. Where's the enjoyment factor, the loving and caring without always being serious?' Where had that come from? No idea, but now that she'd voiced it she knew it was true. Already she was sticking up for her child, like a good mum should.

Hear that, Mum?

Maybe Conor understood the truth because his mouth suddenly softened enough for a smile to appear. A self-deprecating one, but she'd take it as a good sign, a thawing of the chill filling the room and making her skin uncomfortable.

Then he threw another curve ball, and she was back at the beginning. 'What are you hoping for from me? Apart from being there for our...' He choked. 'Our child.' Reality was sinking in deeper and deeper. It was there in his eyes, face, and the way his hands tightened around themselves.

'I hadn't got very far with that. Nor with what I'm going to do about work. Obviously university is a no go.'

'You can always do that later.'

Her eyes did a roll. 'Sure. And spend all those hours studying or training you warned me about away from my child? Never.'

'You're not in this alone.'

Good to know. 'Expand on that if you can.'

'I can't give you specifics yet. Like you, it's still too new to have all the answers, but know that if I'm going to be a dad then I want a full-time role in my child's life.' At last Conor leant back in his recliner, looking more at ease than he had since walking through her door. As though reality was finally falling into line. 'Obviously that means helping you with whatever you decide to do.'

Truly? She ran the words through her mind again and again, searching for the hidden agenda. Nothing waved at her. Either Conor was very good at hiding his true thoughts or... Or he meant what he'd said. 'I've been quite happy living on my own. I adore my job and can adjust to not becoming a doctor. Having a child when I never thought it possible is a far better option anyway.' An opportunity to fill some of those empty spaces within her. Some of those spaces could be for Conor too.

No, they could not.

'You said quite happy. Not good enough, Tamara. You deserve better, lots better.' Then he slammed his hand through that wonderful long hair, shiny black locks weaving between his fingers.

And her fingers stretched, like she needed to feel that hair on her skin. Instead she growled, 'It isn't the life I'd planned on, and while that's not too bad, how I arrived at all this is.'

Apart from that night with you.

'You're letting one man wreck your life. Not to mention tarring the rest of us with the same brush. Not every male is intent on robbing you, or lying to you. Especially not me.'

She had to know. Now, before any further discussion led to decisions regarding their child's future. 'Care to explain what was going on with you in ED this afternoon?' If he couldn't be honest about that then what chance did they have of making this work?

Conor swore. 'Guess I walked into that one.' He unfurled his long body from the chair in one rapid movement and then stopped to stare down at her as if he had no idea where to go from here.

Tamara held his gaze, afraid that if she looked away it would be the end of everything...that he'd find a reason to walk out and send her money once a week via the internet. Honestly? She didn't quite believe that. He was honourable and had said he'd be with her all the way, but history was a hard taskmaster, making her so damned cautious it hurt.

Conor did a lap of the lounge before returning to his chair and locking fierce eyes on her. 'I was having a panic attack.'

She waited. Any questions might shut him down again.

The sound of the building creaking in the cooler night air was loud in the silent room.

And she waited.

'I had a heart attack when I was twenty-two.'

Tamara's jaw dropped. 'You what?' So much for no more questions. They spilled out. 'Twenty-two? But why? You're lean and fit. That's very young for a heart problem.' Seriously? Of course seriously. This wasn't something he'd joke about.

'Family genes have a lot to do with these things.'

Gulp. What? 'You've got an inherited heart disease?'

And she'd thought the worst had been thrown at her already. Shoving her feet to the floor, she sat forward, her hands gripped together between her knees as she waited for his next grenade. And fought the flapping in her stomach. This could not be as bad as it sounded. Huh? Hadn't she learned anything? Life threw grenades at her all the time. What was one more?

'I don't know,' Conor told her.

'But you will be all right? Won't you?' Please. For baby's sake he had to stay around. For her sake. Gulp. Truly? Was she prepared to accept Conor's place in her life as her child's father if it meant he'd never go away? Probably the second biggest mistake of her life but, yes, he had to stay. And not only for the baby. She wanted him there because—because she liked him far too much. Then the truth slammed her.

What if her baby had a heart problem?

CHAPTER SIX

CONOR WATCHED TAMARA closely, but couldn't fault her reaction to his announcement. Nothing but shock and concern in those brown eyes. But she hadn't heard the worst. 'My dad died when I was four.'

Those knees pressed her hands tighter but he'd already seen the tremors roll through her. 'But you're onto it, right? You're not going to die early.'

Conor studied her face, the face that more and more he looked out for first thing in the morning as he logged on in the department. There was something about Tamara he couldn't go past that kept him returning to talk to her and working to raise one of her heart-tugging smiles. Smiles that didn't happen often enough. Hell, she was the only woman in a long time he'd gone to bed with and wanted to repeat the experience. Hence his application for that position in Sydney. He was meant to be a solitary man.

'Yeah, I'm onto it, and I don't intend clocking out early. But there's always that "what if?" factor hovering in the back of my head. Some days, like today when my body was strained from running the marathon and working so hard yesterday, my mind gets in a mess and I freak out, thinking every muscle twinge is a cardiac arrest in progress.'

Had the real issue sunk in yet? Or was Tamara deliberately ignoring it? Somehow he doubted it. She liked honesty and being up front. No doubt a result of what had happened to her in the past.

'What condition have you got?' she asked in a high-pitched squeak.

Conor still wanted to avoid talking about what had kept him single most of his adult life, but he owed Tamara because of their baby. 'Nothing that the cardiologists have been able to put a label on. That's why I can't be sure it is hereditary. But Dad and I both having heart attacks—I'm not prepared to gamble with that information.'

'That must be hard. If you know what you've got it'd be easier to face it down. Or so I'd have thought.'

Got it in one. He smiled; a smile he hoped went some way to lightening the anguish beginning to creep into her eyes as she considered their child might also have a cardiology problem. 'I've learned to live with it by keeping fit, my cholesterol low and my BP normal. Mostly I get on with life without too much interference from the back of my brain, but occasionally it goes haywire. The specialists say my chances of another malfunction are less than most other people's out there because I've got everything under control.'

'Heck, Conor, how do you manage to get up and move, run those marathons even, with that hanging over you?'

By remembering the anguish in Mam's face at Sebastian and Dad's funeral. One funeral, two coffins, two goodbyes. Half the family gone. 'Some things just have to be done, and for me it's running endless kilometres. Don't know what I'll do when the body doesn't want to pound the pavement any more.'

'Take up go-go dancing.' Tamara flicked him an uneasy glance, like she didn't want any more bad news yet had to find out. 'So. Our baby. What are the chances our child will have a heart problem? Is there any way we can find out or do we have to wait until a cardiac event happens?'

She'd got to the crux of the matter. The reason why he'd determined never to have children in the first place. 'I didn't explain properly. My brother didn't die of a heart attack but as the result of being in the car Dad was driving when he had his. The car went over the bridge onto the rocks thirty feet below.'

'That's a rough deal,' she gasped. 'Your poor mother. And you. How did you cope? Hell, Conor, I'm burbling. I don't know what to say. It's awful.'

'Yes, it is. So you'll understand when I said I couldn't have children. There's no way I wanted that happening to my family again.'

'I get that completely. But now you are going to be a dad so we have to talk about our child's medical future.'

He tapped his fingers on the arms of the recliner he sat in. 'It will be a wait-and-see approach for now. Who knows? Medical knowledge is progressing all the time so things could change. But I'll have junior checked by a cardiologist from the moment he's born.' Now he was going with the male thing. 'Or before if it's thought necessary.'

'*We* will.'

'Sorry.' He wasn't used to factoring someone else into his decision-making.

Her hands splayed across her belly. 'We've got knowledge on our side.'

Conor reached for her hands. They were cold and shaky. 'I'll talk to one of the cardiologists in the next couple of weeks. One step at a time, eh?' And he'd keep his fingers crossed all the while that nothing ever went wrong for junior.

'*You'll* talk to someone? Excuse me, buster, but I am as much a part of this as you.'

Conor winced. He'd done it again. 'This is as tricky for me to negotiate as it is for you to take in.'

Tamara nodded as her hands tightened around his. 'I get that.' She gulped. 'I'm afraid.'

His chest felt as though it'd been slammed. Tamara afraid? 'Why?'

Her eyes widened. 'Can I do this?'

'You? Tamara, you'll be amazing.'

'I always wanted children, to have the kind of warm, loving family I grew up in.' Another gulp. 'Until Peter, that is. I got him so wrong. How can I—or you—trust me with a baby? To steer a child through to adulthood? I'm not qualified. I make dreadful decisions.' The words were tumbling out as though she had to say all this fast in case she froze.

Yep, that man had a lot to answer for. This kind, wonderful woman was a blithering wreck behind the confident nurse's façade. 'You're better than that. Don't let him continue winning.'

'I'm trying not to.' Her bottom lip trembled, reminding him of a little girl he'd treated a couple of days ago with a greenstick fracture to her ulna. Only it was Tamara's confidence that was fractured here. And, he suspected, her heart.

He'd have to nurture her, show she was capable of giving love and receiving it back. Huh? Love had nothing to do with their situation. Or did it? He'd been intending to leave Auckland to get away from her, and that hadn't been because he couldn't stand her. But to do that meant getting close. Not happening. 'You don't need qualifications to be a parent, just love and patience and understanding. Kindness. Sympathy. You've got the lot, Tamara.' Conor stood up to pull her to her feet so he could wrap her in a hug. 'Take that determination you had for applying to med school into this new scenario. You can do whatever you want if you don't let the past shackle you.' Definitely do as he said, not as he did.

Her head nodded against his chest. 'I know. Some of the time.'

She fitted so well in his arms, against his length, as though made to be there. Which had nothing to do with their predicament. Or maybe everything to do with it, considering how babies were made. A deep breath in fed his senses with hints of spring and had him softening further into her, holding her tighter, closer. 'You've got me with you on this.'

Tamara shivered, and tension crept into her arms. Too much?

Then his own words whacked him around the skull. He'd just made a commitment he hadn't thought through. So withdraw it. No way. That wasn't how he operated. He did not walk away when life got tough.

You left Ireland when you couldn't face your sisters' happiness, knowing you couldn't join them in family life.

His fingers dragged through his hair. Okay, so what? He wasn't leaving Tamara to face raising the baby on her own. Neither would he ever desert his child. Hell, now he was going to be a dad he should be looking forward to embracing the whole deal.

She told him, 'We'll keep a fierce watch over our child.'

Conor slowly let his arm fall away and stepped back. 'I don't want to repeat what happened to my brother.'

Those sweet, generous arms were back around him, and this time he was the one being pulled close. 'Conor, you're tormenting yourself over something you can't control. I understand that's why you've opted not to have a family but that's changed.' The words were whispered against his throat and were followed with a feather-light kiss. Then Tamara stood still, holding him, letting him hold her, as they absorbed strength and comfort from each other. At least he hoped he was giving Tamara as good as she gave him, because it felt right, and she needed good as much as he did.

Finally, as though there'd been a signal, they stepped apart and sat down in their respective chairs. Conor watched Tam closely, glad to see nothing to suggest she wanted him gone, out of the picture because of his history. He risked, 'We'll sort all this out but no more tonight. We're both exhausted.' He still needed to get his head around the fact he was going to be a dad. And then there were decisions to make. Only that morning he'd had an email from Sydney about a second interview for the job—this time face to face. The job he'd been excited about and still wanted.

'At least I'm not on my own.' Relief warred with worry in that brown gaze fixed on him.

Hopefully Tam would move to Australia with him if he got the job. That would solve everything about how to jointly raise their child. 'You've told no one else you're pregnant? Not even Kelli?' When she shook her head he asked, 'What about your mother?'

Her face tightened, and she sat up straighter. 'We don't communicate.'

'At all?' Didn't sound like there were many people in Tamara's life to support her.

'I tried tonight. She hung up the moment I said hello. That's how it works with us.'

'Because of what happened with your fiancé?'

Her nod was sharp. 'Mum was so hurt by it all.'

As her daughter had been. Conor smiled into that worried face and changed the subject to something lighter. They'd had more than enough doom and gloom for one night. 'Have you eaten?'

A blush crept up her cheeks. 'Ah, no. I could go for a pizza delivery right now. All I had today were those pastries for lunch.'

Yes. Her eyes were lightening, the mud shade beginning to sparkle just a little bit, reminding him of cocoa this time. He hadn't realised how much he'd needed to see that twinkle and how special it was when it happened.

'Your propensity for takeout food's interesting. Going to feed baby on Indian curries before he's twelve months old?' More than once he'd seen her hoeing into a korma at lunchtime in the department.

'If it's good enough for Indians to bring their children up on spicy food, it's got to work for mine.' Now the sparkle was at full wattage.

On the inside he was melting, giving in to the wonderful sensations suggesting he might've found his soul mate. Suggesting he might not turn tail and hide from happiness. 'You should bottle that look.'

'What?' Puzzlement tipped her mouth awry, and he just had to lean over to kiss her. To seal the day with a kiss? To show her they were on the same page? Two kisses. They hadn't even started sorting all the obstacles in front of them. Three.

As his lips brushed hers again he felt her pushing closer, and deepening the kiss was a natural follow-up. Afraid she'd tip onto the floor, he grabbed her and lifted her onto his thighs. She was acting as if she wanted more, despite all her misgivings. Because she had plenty, that was obvious. Well, he was going to do all he could to see her through some of them, to banish or work them out of her system. She deserved someone on her side. Someone to bat for her, to hold her when the going got too tough. Someone who still had to figure out what had been dropped on him, and changed his world for ever. Right now he had no energy for thinking.

If you had to get stuck in the pregnancy situation then you couldn't have picked a better, more gorgeous woman to be there with.

Conor straightened. Whoa! Where had that come from?

'What's wrong?' Tamara asked as she tipped back against him, her fingers tracing her lips where he'd been placing those kisses.

Kisses he'd love to follow up on. To turn away from their problems and lose themselves in each other. But nothing would've changed, might even be harder to work through if they did that. Could have him aiming for the moon, and not only working to make everything okay for their baby. Hauling the brakes on his libido, he answered her question. 'Nothing, absolutely nothing.'

Disbelief filled her eyes. 'What are you on, buster?'

'Adrenalin.'

Another aspect of Tamara filled his mind as he looked across at her. Laughing, sexy, fun Tamara letting her hair down with him as they made love. And they'd made a baby apparently. The tension in his stomach turned to goo. He was going to be a dad. The decision had been taken away from him and now he had to go with it. Could go with it and imagine the excitement. Let it in.

I want to go with it.

'I'm going to be a father.' The love winding through him was beyond description. For so long he'd refused to contemplate becoming a parent and now it was happening regardless. So, yes, he was starting to see it for the wonderful opportunity it was. Not that he was foolish enough to believe the worry wouldn't be huge, hold him down at times, but Tamara had been right to point out there was more to becoming a parent than the apprehension.

'Weren't we talking about food?' Her practical question knocked him back into the here and now of finishing their day on a normal note.

'Yes, and I'm starving.'

'I can't wait for a pizza delivery. There's some steak and things to make a salad in the fridge.'

'Let's hit it.' He hadn't had dinner either, having been too wound up and needing to have everything out with Tamara to think about eating. 'I'll cook the steak. I don't do a bad job.'

'Go for it. There's a barbecue at the back door, though I'm not sure if it works. I've never used it. Hardly seemed worth the effort for one small piece of meat.'

'What's the alternative?'

'A heavy pan on the element.'

'That'll do.'

In the kitchen Tamara was opening cupboards, lifting out a pan, plates, salad bowl. All top-of-the-range equipment.

'You have excellent taste in furnishings and utilities,' he noted as he opened the fridge to find the steak.

'They came from my parents' home. I helped myself to enough to furnish this place before the courts placed a "to be sold" order on everything. But even then I think I'd have got away with going back for extras if I'd wanted. The receivers were more than kind to me after they heard what had happened. They didn't believe I deserved to be thrown out in the street on my butt with absolutely nothing but the shoes I was wearing. By then they'd had time to study the business affairs and follow the money trail.'

Placing the steak on the bench, he went in search of cooking oil in the pantry. Go for serious or fun? 'I'm trying to get around the vision of you sitting naked in the street wearing only a pair of shoes. It's quite a sight, believe me.'

'The neighbours mightn't have approved.' Tamara's laughter filled the room, pulled them together in a cosy, let's-be-normal kind of way.

Except it wasn't normal for him. He didn't share his kitchen with anyone. Or his lounge or bedroom. Tamara had been the only woman he'd taken back there.

'Bet they would. You forget I've seen that butt and it's quite something.' Not that he wanted to share the experience with anyone else. Didn't want another man knocking on Tamara's door anytime. Down, boy. Keep to the cosy and cook the steak.

'Tell me more about your family.' Tamara was chopping a red onion at a frenzied rate that had no consistency behind it.

Fearing for her fingers, Conor placed his hand on her wrist. 'Stop, woman. You're going to do yourself an injury at that rate.' He tugged the knife free and began systematically dicing the onion. 'What else do you want sliced?'

'All of these.' She placed tomatoes, cucumber, capsicum, a carrot and celery on the bench before digging through the vegetable bin again.

'The steak's on hold while I do this.'

'You worry too much. I've been chopping vegetables for years and still got all ten digits.'

He turned to her question about his family. 'I've got four half-sisters and they're all bonkers. I adore them, and wouldn't swap them for a saner variety.'

'That's cool. Are their kids normal or—' she made finger quotes '—"bonkers"?'

'Still up for debate. The brothers-in-law are leaning towards bonkers, but they're not fazed either way. The kids' ages range from two to seven. They're so much fun. So cute and crazy.' Oh, hell. The chopping stopped as he stared across the kitchen at Tamara. 'I—we—are going to be adding to the Maguire brood. There're going to be five grandkids for Mum to spoil.'

Tamara stilled, a pair of kitchen tongs in one hand, some mushrooms in the other. 'Is that all right?' Caution laced her question.

'It's more than all right. It's— It's wonderful.' It really was.

As long as baby's heart is fine.

Conor shivered. Go away. Let me enjoy the moment.

'It *is* going to be all right.' Tamara stood in front of him, her hands on his upper arms. 'We're in this together.'

'But—'

'But tonight we're going to share a meal, acknowledge we're going to be parents and just take in the wonder of that. There's plenty of time to worry about what might or might not happen.' She shook him gently. 'Okay?'

'That's how I want to play it, if only this pesky little voice in my head would leave me alone.' He was getting to share parts of him he'd never told anyone about. Not a good sign for his independence.

Tamara wagged a finger between them. 'Pesky little voice, go annoy someone else. Tonight is ours. Not yours.'

Laughter began deep in his belly and rolled up and out between them. What a tonic she was. If he had to have anyone onside if things went bad then Tamara was who he wanted, needed. 'How do you like your steak?'

Tamara placed her empty dinner plate on the floor beside her chair and watched Conor as he finished his meal. Letting him kiss her had been wrong. Kissing him back worse. But there hadn't been a stop-go man in her lounge, flipping his sign back and forth. Just her and Conor. Tired, and temporarily at ease with each other, needing to keep the truce running for as long as possible, she had to ignore the flare of need that kiss had evoked. The need that refused to die down even though they'd stopped kissing ages ago.

Why had Conor ended the kiss? His withdrawal had been gentle, but had left her depleted when everything sensible in her head—okay, not a lot—had shouted at her, *Don't do it*! She had so much to lose. More than ever before. Yet her body had craved him, her mouth devoured his taste, her arms desperate to be wound around him, holding him. She'd made a baby with this man. Her body remembered every little detail, every spin of desire, every heightened sensation, the exquisite release of that night.

She wanted it again. Needed to connect with him in a deep, intimate way that showed they had made a baby together, that this was real. That it wasn't another lie thrown at her by people she'd trusted.

Already she was beginning to believe, really believe deep inside that Conor meant every word he'd said so far about being there for her, not against her. Giving in too easily? Because she desperately wanted a man at her side to go through her pregnancy and the years to follow with? A man? Any man? No. Conor. If there was going to be someone at her side then Conor was the only man she'd consider. But they had hardly touched base on the issues ahead. That's when her burgeoning belief in him might step back.

'You're awfully quiet over there,' the man making her brain do somersaults said. 'Should I be worrying about something?' Conor looked so relaxed and at ease her own tension lightened somewhat.

'No.' Yes. He'd have a fit if he knew what she'd been thinking. 'Just putting the day into perspective.' Some of it, anyway. The tantalising part, the warm sizzle component of a long day fraught with landmines.

Conor hauled himself out of the recliner. 'I'm off home so you get some shut-eye.'

'That's probably best.' Unfortunately. She followed him to the front door, her heart getting heavier with every step, lonelier with every breath.

With his hand on the doorknob Conor hesitated. 'Goodnight, Tam.'

She sucked a breath, bit down on the automatic 'Don't', and whispered, 'Conor.'

He shifted his hand to her neck to gently pull her closer to his face, his mouth hovering above hers. His other arm went around her waist, brought her against his wide chest. Then he was kissing her. Again. And she was sagging with relief. And firing up with desire. 'Hold me tighter.'

Her lower body pressed in against him, felt his reaction behind his zip. Her hips rocked forward. Conor froze. Great. His head was at odds with his body. Of course he didn't want her. She'd made another mistake. She pulled away. 'Sorry. I got that wrong.'

'Tam, I have no idea what's right or wrong at the moment. I only know I want to be with you tonight. I understand it's asking a lot, considering what's lying between us. But tonight…' He lifted his shoulders. 'Tonight I want to remember what was so good between us last time, and forget everything else for a few hours.'

Was that so bad? It was what she wanted too. 'Stay.' Tamara touched his chin, his cheek and then traced his lips. 'Stay.'

Feed the heat devouring me…feel the wetness waiting for you.

Before she could blink he'd swung her up into his arms and was heading for her bedroom.

At the door he hesitated. 'You're sure?' He was holding his breath. If she changed her mind she knew he'd leave.

She placed her lips on his neck, right beneath his ear at a sensitive spot she'd discovered last time with him. Her tongue licked and teased his skin. A deep shudder racked him, and he responded by placing her on her feet and sliding his hands under her blouse and up to her breasts. A flick of his thumbs across her nipples and her desire level shot from simmer to boiling. Once had never been enough with Conor.

With their mouths joined they somehow shucked out of their clothes, breaking contact only to haul shirts over their heads. Then they were on the bed, sprawled across each other, hands touching, teasing, awakening deep needs.

'This is one hell of a way to say yes,' he croaked as his knee slid between her thighs and nudged her wide. His eyes were hazy with lust and the same need that was scalding her on the inside.

Tamara opened up to Conor, exposing herself completely, letting his body join hers, his gaze see right into her. To see her truth, fears and hopes. Hopes she hadn't allowed herself for so long.

Her fingers pushed through his hair, tension growing in the fingertips that pummelled his skull. Her breasts ached with need and she throbbed at her core. Then Conor slid into her, and wiped away the day, the problems and the worry. Left her mindless and replete.

CHAPTER SEVEN

'WHO'S THE NEW man in Tamara Washington's life? No one's saying but at Auckland Central Hospital—'

Tamara slammed the clock radio so hard it spun off the bedside table. 'Shut up,' she cried.

'Hey, take it easy.' Conor sat up beside her and draped an arm over her shoulder. 'You're letting them win.'

'Don't you get it? The new man? That's you they're talking about.' How did the reporters know Conor had anything to do with her? Even *she* didn't think they were an item, baby excepted. Another hot night excepted... 'They've been hanging around my flat again.' Bitterness spilled into her mouth. What would the reporters have to say when her baby bump became apparent?

That arm on her shoulders increased its pressure as Conor shuffled closer. 'You think reporters saw me arrive here last night? Hung around to see if I left?'

'That's how it works in my life.' Damn them all to hell and back. 'This round started with that photo of us working with the children in ED. I'm sorry. I totally get it if you only want to meet at work or with the shift guys when we go to the pub after hours.' Conor didn't deserve her mistakes being played out in his life.

Before she knew what Conor was doing she was on her back with him above her, his elbows framing her, his hands holding her head gently. 'We're going to ignore them. I won't hide away because some reporters have nothing better to do with their time. They'll get bored with me soon enough.' His mouth covered hers, preventing her from retorting that they hadn't forgotten her in years, and she wasn't half as exciting as Conor.

As Conor's kiss deepened she gave in to the warmth that expanded through her chilled body; forgot everything but the man delivering it. Spreading her hands across his chest, she absorbed his strength through her palms, and understood she was safe when she was with Conor. When she rubbed a finger across his nipple he groaned, long and low, and she wanted more. The whole deal. Making love in the morning was different from any other time. It came with sleep-lazy bodies waking up to a new day together, with promise for more, with a languidness that wasn't there at the end of a busy day.

Conor touched her thighs, nudged her legs wide, and then she wasn't languid any more.

'We're going to be late for work,' she murmured as she grasped him in her hand.

'I can do fast.' He chuckled and immediately proved his point. What's more, he was very good at it.

When they walked into work Tamara knew she shouldn't be smiling like she'd had chocolate for breakfast. Face it, she hadn't had anything for breakfast.

Not true. She'd had Conor.

Conor and chocolate. Hmm.

Chocolate. Food. Yikes. Stomach not happy. 'Excuse me.' She dashed away, leaving Kelli, who'd just joined them, staring after her.

'What's going on?' Kelli asked as she followed her to

the bathroom. 'Why didn't you stay home if you were feeling…?' Her voice trailed away. 'Oh. I get it.'

Tamara closed her ears to that sound of astonished comprehension in her friend's voice. She had an annoying stomach to deal with first.

Then Conor was there. 'Need anything, Tamara?'

Yes, to be left in peace for a moment. 'I'm fine.'

'You reckon?' Kelli squeaked.

'It's normal,' Conor grunted.

'Will you both go away?' Tamara called through the door. 'This isn't exactly fun to be sharing with the pair of you.' But it seemed her stomach had decided to behave, probably more interested in the conversation than heaving. Out at the basin she splashed cold water over her face.

'Here.' Conor blotted up the trickles from her chin and cheeks with a hand towel.

While Kelli gaped at him, then her, then back at Conor. 'I think I've missed something. I know I said you should let your hair down, Tamara, but it seems your knickers were what came down.' Then her face split into a big grin. 'Go, girlfriend.' Then the grin vanished. 'Are you all right? Is Conor doing the right thing by you?'

As Conor spun to face her friend Tamara stepped between them. 'All's good, Kelli. Promise. I'm sorry I haven't told you anything but it's been a bit tricky.'

'I take it this news is not up for grabs out in the department.'

'No.'

'Not yet,' muttered Conor.

'Then we'd better get out of here before people start asking dumb questions.' Kelli led the way from the tiny room.

Yeah, Kelli was the greatest friend she had, and could ever wish for. Of course she was the only one. But she'd just been delivered news that'd have her reeling and yet there'd been no criticism, or any hurt feelings about not having been told earlier. Tamara slipped her arm around her waist. 'You're the best.'

Kelli returned the gesture. 'You bet.' Then her face clouded. 'How are you really? Getting back in the saddle is one thing, but a baby? With a guy you hardly know outside work?'

The happiness evaporated. 'I'm all over the place about it,' she muttered. 'I believe Conor when he says he's on my side, and then the past springs up and I'm afraid of what he can do to me.'

'You're not ready for this.'

Tamara huffed out a lungful of despair. 'Tell me something I don't know.' How could she have spent last night making love with Conor when they hadn't got anywhere with working out plans for the future? She'd given in to her physical needs too easily. Given in to Conor too easily. Hadn't found the strength to say no. Hard to do when her body was screaming for him to take her. 'Guess I haven't changed half as much as I'd hoped.'

'We'll talk later.' Kelli gave her a lopsided smile and tipped her head in warning towards the group waiting in the middle of ED for handover from the night shift.

Talk later. Hadn't she heard those words earlier today from Conor? Seemed her immediate future was going to be filled with talking. About her baby, Conor, the future. Time to lay out what she hoped for, not sit back and see what Conor would offer. This time she had to fight for the needs of her baby, not fold, or let anyone else determine how the next year, years were going to play out. Doing that would only prove she hadn't learnt a thing. And that she wasn't fit to be a mother. Not happening. Her vertebrae clicked as she lifted her head high.

I have changed. I am strong. I will not let any man dic-tate the rest of my life.

She had to learn to trust herself first, and then every-thing might fall into place more easily with Conor.

'Two car accidents during the night.' The day began. 'There's still one patient from the second incident here under observation with severe concussion but no other injuries.'

'Kelli, he's yours.' Conor nodded.

'Cubicle seven. Fifty-six-year-old female, fell down the stairs around midnight. Concussion, broken arm, bruis-ing to her face and upper body.' Nothing major enough to still be here.

'What's the problem?' Conor asked.

The registrar leading handover said, 'Her husband doesn't believe his wife drinks, yet her bloods showed a very high reading. He blames the lab for the results.'

'Had he been out for the evening and not known?' Ta-mara asked as she focused on work and nothing else.

'Nope. Her liver tests were abnormal. I'd suggest that's from a high and sustained alcohol intake.'

'So the husband's playing ostrich,' Conor noted.

The registrar added, 'I'm concerned about sending her home.'

'I'll talk to Social Services when their offices open.' Conor looked around, caught her eye. 'Tamara, I want you on this one.'

'Not a problem.'

It was like any other day in ED. But for Tamara it *was* different. Everywhere she went Conor was there, whether it was him or his voice through the curtains or his laughter as he chatted with other staff. Once she even smelt his spicy aftershave when she entered a cubicle he'd just vacated. Her body wouldn't settle down, as though her hormones had got a taste for Conor that had to be fed at regular intervals. Sure made working beside him awkward. And thrilling. This time Conor was responsible for her inability to eat, not baby.

The buzzer sounded.

'Tamara, can you take that?' Conor nudged her out of her reverie as he walked past, flicking her one of those smiles she adored.

And, yes, cranked up the desire level. 'Sure.' The man could ask her to do anything when he smiled like that. He oozed charm.

Charm? As in used to getting his own way? Was this all just a ruse to soften her up before he explained how he was going to deal with her and their baby? Tamara shivered, rubbed her hands up and down her arms. Please, not that. One Peter in her life was one too many.

No. Conor was nothing like her ex. Conor was genuinely kind, caring, honourable. Gorgeous, sexy. Oh, and sexy.

But… What if she was wrong? What if he was laying out plans for her already?

No. He wouldn't. He'd told her so.

'Peter Gillespie is a hard-working man with your and my interests at heart. He'll always look out for you and Washington Engineering.'

So had said her father as he'd pushed documents in front of her to sign that would give her control over the company and its finances once he knew his mind was going because of the dementia.

'He'll explain everything to you before you sign any papers. You can trust him completely.'

Yeah, Dad, thanks for that.

Yeah, Dad, I miss you like it all happened yesterday.

Tonight she'd look into the laws covering a mother's rights. Only being a responsible parent.

* * *

In the end Conor had to let the woman with alcohol issues go home. There were no grounds for keeping her in ED, and no other ward would take her. Alcoholism, a broken arm and an unkind husband were not reasons for admittance.

He'd forwarded the details to the woman's GP with his concerns and to Social Services after talking to them. Then he got on with the day, treating a steady stream of patients coming through the doors.

For the last hour Tamara seemed intent on avoiding him, swapping from cases he was on as often as possible. Too often for his liking. Seemed that morning's cosy mood had gone, replaced by apprehension and long, questioning looks that didn't give him confidence in their upcoming discussions.

Conor had seen her yawning far too often. The pregnancy was taking its toll. Nothing to do with a very physical night, of course. He winced. Tam had been more than willing to make love last night. And this morning. Yet now she was treating him like she would a white-tailed spider.

An ache stabbed him under the ribs. Unfair. But he had to be patient. Give her time and space to get used to him in the role of father to her baby and hopefully someone she would learn to rely on in the coming weeks and years. To love him? Seriously? No, that was going too far. He couldn't ask more of her than he was prepared to give. Love meant sharing their lives, losing his freedom to do as he pleased, always having to check with Tamara before doing things he normally just went and did. He wasn't sure he knew how to do that. Or wanted to. But the baby was going to give him a few lessons along the way.

'You know you're going to be on the news tonight?' Tamara nudged him during one quiet interlude.

That's why Tamara couldn't let go enough to trust him completely. The past was still in her face, refusing to go away. He replied, 'If that's all people have got to make their day, they're the ones with problems, not me.'

As reporters jostled for position in front of them when they'd walked down her path to his car that morning, his rare temper had leapt to the fore. At least he'd managed to hang onto it. One look at the resignation in Tamara's face and he'd known not to react, not give the media what they wanted. Ignoring every one of them, he'd been rewarded with Tamara holding her head high like she didn't care about what they'd write. 'We did all right this morning.'

'You haven't thought it through. Everyone here's going to start talking about us.'

'Then let's fix that. We'll announce it ourselves.'

'Announce what?' she gasped, the colour draining from her cheeks. 'The baby?'

'Why not? You won't be able to hide it for much longer. Personally I'd prefer for it to be out in the open.'

'I'm not ready for that,' she snapped. 'I've only just told you, and we—we haven't planned anything yet.' Tamara pulled that frightened look away from him but left him with a sense of having betrayed her somehow.

Guess he had. He hadn't asked her how she felt about telling others. 'Hey.' He stepped close.

A hand went up between them in the universal stop sign. 'I can't believe you'd suggest such a thing.'

Now what? *Think, man.* What was behind this? Tamara was rattled big time. Calm her down, get her back on her feet so she can face her colleagues without going into another meltdown. 'Fair enough. We won't mention the baby yet. But we can say we've spent some time together and are continuing to do so. Sounds a bit like a press release from the rich and famous.' Hell. That's what she was used to, had had to put up with before. 'I'll reword that.'

That thick blonde braid swung across her back from shoulder to shoulder. 'They'll understand.' She headed for the ambulance bay, though there'd been no sign of a patient arriving.

Conor followed, reluctant to let her go on a bad note. 'Since we've got lots to discuss, want to do it over a meal tonight?' As in a real date.

Hope warred with resignation across her face when she turned to look at him. 'I don't think so.'

'With what's ahead we should be getting to know each other better.' Next he'd be down on his knees, begging her to spend time with him. Only went to show how his thinking had changed since hearing about the baby. 'Say yes. We've got to eat anyway.'

'We've spent the last two evenings together and haven't got around to the big issues. Why would tonight be any different?'

'We won't have had an eventful day to use up all our energy?' *Tempting fate, buster.* He continued when she wasn't forthcoming with a reply. 'Are you changing your mind about my role in our baby's life?'

Guilt flickered. 'I don't know exactly what your role's going to be.'

Got you. 'Then we need to go out to dinner and talk. Before we get much further along the track.' Try asking, not pushing. 'Please?'

One eyebrow rose, but she only stared at him.

'Have you tried that new Indian restaurant on K Road?'

'Low blow, Dr Maguire.'

'Did it work?'

A shrug. Then a tiny, reluctant smile full of caution. 'What time are you picking me up?'

She didn't trust him. Despite everything he'd said. Despite showing her with his lovemaking. It was going to take time. And that sucked.

Could she want more from him? The boundaries he'd lived with were coming down because of a baby. His baby. And because of this amazing woman who'd first tipped his world a little bit sideways, and was now following up with a big shove just by revealing more about herself. He wanted to support her, stand by her and deal with the past, and not just for the baby's sake. As long as he could do it without losing his heart, without giving up that solitude he'd struggled to maintain. The solitude that kept him safe. And which had begun cracking wide open these past few days. And since he no longer needed to push Tamara away. Conor shivered. Hell, did he want the whole deal after all?

I'm not falling in love with Tamara.

No, he wasn't. Spending more time with her had grown on him, and not to discuss nappies and baby formula. Was that love? Creeping in to bang him around the skull now that he had no excuse to keep his distance? He was going to be a parent regardless of his family history so why not pursue the other half of that picture? The mother of his child. Tam. The woman who'd had him aiming to move to another country because she'd woven a spell around him when he hadn't thought it possible.

Because it still wasn't. Or was it? Spending time together might resolve some of the dread lurking in his head. Might displace the fear of hurting Tamara if his family history roared into life and left her alone with their child.

'I'll have the lamb dhansak.' Tamara looked up at the waitress. 'Hot.'

The only way to eat curry. She shrugged out of her faded denim jacket and dropped it on the back of her chair.

It had seen too many wears, the threads barely holding together at the elbows. But, hey, it matched her scuffed ballet shoes.

'Butter chicken, mild, for me,' Conor ordered, before asking her, 'You don't worry all that chilli might upset junior?'

'He'll probably come out with a taste for spices, which would be great.'

'Where does this enjoyment of Indian food come from?'

'I had a friend at school, Savita, and I spent many weekends at her house.' Until Sav's family had packed up and moved to Melbourne for family reasons. 'At first I wouldn't eat anything except naan bread but Mrs Kesry was very patient and drip-fed me spicy food, increasing the chilli slowly, until the day came when I could eat whatever Savita ate.'

'You'll need to be as patient with me.'

'We're going to spend that much time together?' Did she want to? Absolutely. When she wasn't feeling uncertain about him she wanted nothing more than to be with Conor. They'd spent three nights in a row together and were still on friendly terms. Had to be a good start.

'We're going to be parents. Don't they have a lot to discuss and share and enjoy together?'

'You're giving back my comments from yesterday.' She liked that. They were on the same page for tonight. 'Right, curry training starts now.'

'You're not going to change my order?'

'I have the power.' She laughed. It felt good to laugh. Something she did more often when around Conor. He was good for her. When she wasn't doubting herself.

'Please, please, don't be harsh on me. I'll tell junior in years to come how cruel his mother can be.'

Junior. *His* mother. Tamara folded her hands in her lap

and took a big breath. 'Do you want to find out if junior is a boy? I should be seeing the midwife anyway and he's going to suggest a scan.'

'He? A male midwife?' Conor's eyelids were doing some rapid movements.

'You didn't know there's such a creature?' she teased.

'Yes, of course I do. Just hadn't considered it.' He shifted in his chair.

'So I'll make an appointment with *him*?'

'If it's a boy, you're going to be outnumbered right from the start.'

'That's a yes, then.' Tamara tapped in a reminder on her phone. Not that she was likely to forget but best to cover all contingencies.

'Are you intending to continue living in the flat once the baby is born?'

So he wasn't offering to set up home with her. 'I don't have anywhere else to go. Besides, I like it there. It's not flash or big but I'm comfortable.' There wasn't money to rent a house. The money she'd put aside for next year at university would be used for her current level of rent, and all the other things to buy, such as a cot, pram and change table, a car that would be safe for a baby. That was only the beginning. She had no doubt the list would be endless over the coming years.

'Fair enough.' Conor sipped his water, looking distinctly uncomfortable.

'What?' Was he about to lob a bomb? Make demands she wouldn't accept? Because it was his child? 'What?' she demanded again in a higher pitch.

Draining the glass, he set it down with precision then lifted his gaze to her. 'My role as a father.'

Here we go. Tamara's stomach tightened, as though

holding baby closer. As she waited to be slammed, her breath caught in her lungs.

'I want a part in my child's life.'

'I expected that, and want it too.'

'You sound wary.'

'Not at all,' she fibbed.

'Oh, hell, I'm worrying you sick, aren't I? You've warned me about your lack-of-trust issues and I'm walking all over them.' Conor leaned closer. 'I'm trying to start a discussion about how we're going to manage parenting from two different homes, and, if I stick to my plans, from two different countries, unless you come with me.'

That stalled breath limped across her lips as she accepted his explanation for what it appeared to be. 'I don't have to stay in Auckland.'

'I don't have to move to Sydney.' His head jerked back as though he'd just shocked himself. 'I haven't had my final interview yet. It's been put back for another two weeks as one of the doctors involved had to take an urgent trip to New York. I'm one of two they're considering so if I pull out they'll save time and expense.'

'If you really want the job, then go.' She hesitated, straightened her spine mentally and physically, and stepped into the abyss. 'I can join you over there. I'd get a job easily enough, I imagine.'

'You'd do that?'

Hadn't she just said so? 'I'm not suggesting we live together. I wouldn't ask that of you.'

Male pride flipped into his face. 'Why not? We get on okay. Or don't you agree?'

Embarrassment flooded her. 'I meant I wasn't proposing a couple-type relationship.'

Proposing? Tamara Washington, wash your mouth out. 'We could share accommodation and the baby.'

'She wounds so easily.' He hadn't quite banished the wounded-pride look but it was lifting.

The heat in her cheeks heightened to an inferno. 'This isn't easy for me,' Tamara muttered, wishing the floor would open beneath her.

'Seems to me you're doing great.' Conor refilled their glasses with iced water. 'You only said what I was getting around to in a haphazard kind of way. Sharing an apartment or house is a good solution to joint parenting. I don't mind if we share a bedroom too. I mean…' he shrugged '…we do get along in that department. Very well, in my view.'

Okay, floor, hold that opening for a moment. 'You want to live with me and our baby? As in a couple kind of relationship?' Was that what she wanted?

'Why the surprise?'

'It never occurred to me. You have a busy social life and I'm sure I wasn't the first woman you took back to your apartment after a night on the town. A baby. And me. We'd cramp your style.' What a good idea. The thought of Conor with another woman didn't sit comfortably.

He had the cheek to laugh. 'You think? You were the only woman in my apartment, in my bed, and before you suggest I've got a problem I probably have, just not the one you're thinking.'

She hadn't been thinking. It was too hard, and confusing. But tension backed off as his words hit home. She'd been the last woman he'd made love with. Yes! Slow down. It was too soon to be getting excited. She wasn't completely convinced she could trust her judgement yet.

He continued. 'We had a wonderful night together and it started me wondering if I was missing out on something. Then I'd remind myself of my pledge never to marry.'

'Is that why you left Ireland? There was someone you

were serious about?' She'd walk away now if that was the case.

'I left because every time I was with my sisters and their families, the pain of what I couldn't have overwhelmed me. I wanted it so badly, yet asking someone to take that risk with me was impossible.'

'You chose not to marry because of what happened to your brother and dad. Why couldn't you have gone with no children and still married?'

'I couldn't ask a woman to give up having a family for me.' He even had a smile on that gorgeous mouth.

But since she'd got pregnant with *his* baby, he could ask her to join him because it was all too late. She was the soft option. He'd have the child he longed for and a woman who knew the score and couldn't walk away because of that child. Thanks a million. Tamara's heart sank. She definitely needed to delve further into what made Conor tick.

Conor was watching her as he forked up a mouthful of butter chicken and rice. 'One week at a time, Tamara.'

One week? One day was difficult enough. Tamara tried following his example with her meal but swallowing became impossible as she waited for what he'd say next.

Finally he put the fork down. 'That's seriously delicious.'

Her throat opened and her food went down—without the enjoyment factor. What was going on? Was Conor toying with her? Or, 'Am I expecting too much of you?'

'What *do* you want from me, Tamara?' Conor's query stilled the questions in her mind.

'I didn't know what you'd do about—'

'The question is what do *you want* of me? When you knew you had to tell me about the baby, what were you expecting? A cash handout? A home? Me to walk away? To stay and support you? What?'

The truth and only the truth. Not that she'd worked everything out, but she would start as of now. 'Firstly, your support.' She drew a tick in the air. 'Got it in spades.'

'Yes, you have.'

'Secondly, that you'll always be there for your child, that he'd grow up knowing you, having you in his life for real and not a phone call or email away.'

'You even doubted that?' he growled.

'A little.' His face didn't lighten up. 'How was I to know? You were planning on moving to Australia, often commented about how settling down wasn't for you when others at work talked about buying a house or moving in with a partner. I didn't know why you move around. Now I wonder if you're aware of what you're getting into, how it's going to cramp your style.'

'I applied for that position in Sydney because I was starting to feel close to you. I had to put space between us, forget you.'

This guy was good at curve balls. She waited for her heart to stop the tap dance it was doing before saying, 'So you're open to settling down somewhere.' She wouldn't delve into what else he'd implied. Too tricky when she was trying to be level-headed.

'Yes. Believe me when I say I take this seriously and my son or daughter will always be a major part of my life, regardless of what you and I decide to do about a relationship.'

Her forefinger traced another tick. 'Thank you.'

Shifting his butt and draping his arm over the back of the chair, Conor nodded. 'Carry on.'

'I'd like the happy family scene if at all possible. I grew up safe and happy. Dad adored me, spoilt me rotten. Not so sure about my mum, though.'

Mum, you need to know I'm pregnant. There are so

many things I want to tell you. Neither should you miss out on anything to do with your grandchild.

Conor nodded. 'Family is most important. Losing my dad was horrific, and I was a lost wee soul until the man who became my stepdad came along.'

'How do we make it work? It's not like we're in a relationship already.' They barely knew each other outside work and bed.

Now he locked his gaze on her. 'Look at how we're dealing with this. We know each other professionally, got on very well the night we spent at my apartment and the world didn't implode when you told me about the pregnancy. I reckon we're off to a better start than some.'

'You make it sound straightforward.' The warning bells were tolling. Was she being sucked in again?

'I don't mean to, and yet in a way I do.' He pushed his now empty plate aside, and reached for her hand. 'I want this, Tamara. More than anything. You, me and the baby. I've been given an opportunity I never believed I'd have, and I want to make certain we get it right. It's a chance for something special I don't want to stuff up or lose.'

Couldn't be more blunt than that. This was about the baby and how to jointly make it work. Not about them and love and any of those crazy things. Which was fine, considering she couldn't trust her heart either. 'Sydney or Auckland?' she asked.

Conor looked a little shocked. No doubt the enormity of what they'd agreed to was only beginning to sink in. 'Leave that to me for now.'

Those alarm bells clanged harder. 'A partnership, remember? You can't cut me out of any decisions that involve me or the baby.'

He winced. 'It's a work in progress, okay?'

'Not good enough.'

'You have to believe I'll do the right thing by all of us, Tamara.'

'The thing is…' Oh, grow up. Take responsibility. Give the guy a break. He hadn't put a foot wrong yet, but he also hadn't made it easy for her about everything. 'I do. Just don't exclude me from decisions, okay?'

CHAPTER EIGHT

CONOR BLINKED, THEN stared at the apparition walking into the department.

Tamara in fitted scrubs. Scrubs that showcased the perfect figure wearing them. Wow. She looked stunning.

Down, boyo. You're at work.

True. And if Tam knew what was in his mind she'd do the aloof thing all morning. But… A guy was allowed to dream, wasn't he? It was the end of the week, and who knew what they might get up to in the weekend? 'Morning, Tam.'

She didn't even bite. Just tightened her hands into fists as she walked towards him. 'Hi.'

Make-up. Her face was always beautiful. Today he was all out of words. Those deep brown eyes, accentuated with mascara and some other coloured goo, were bigger, brighter, more fall-into-them-looking. Her peaky cheeks had colour, her lips… How could he not have been aware they were so full? So luscious? It was going to be a very long day.

Tam came around the end of the counter and stood in front of him. 'You still on for four o'clock?'

Blink. 'Of course I am,' he snapped. 'Like I'd bail.'

'I was thinking more that you might have to stay back to do paperwork or something.'

At the end of most days he usually put in an hour behind his desk, trying to placate the paper gods upstairs. 'Not today. Our—'

She cut him off with a warning nod to the side. 'Morning, guys.'

The day crew had arrived all together. 'Later.' He gave Tam a curt nod. Damn but she looked beyond beautiful. Not even her permanent exhaustion was getting a look in this morning.

A registrar from the previous shift filled them in on patients before heading away.

Conor's nostrils received a hit of spring flowers. Tamara stood beside him. He breathed deeper, enjoyed the scent, remembered her satin-like skin, and forced his body to behave.

A gentle nudge from Tamara's elbow.

When he glanced sideways he fell into a huge smile.

An almost imperceptible shake of her head. She knew what he was thinking?

Then Michael stood up. 'Hope everyone can join me at the local after work. It's my birthday on Sunday so I'm shouting a few rounds.'

'Sorry, but I've got an appointment at four.' One he wouldn't miss for anything. Excitement fizzed in his veins.

'You can't change it?' Michael asked. 'I know you won't be drinking since you're running that race tomorrow but they sell water.'

'No can do.' Conor stared straight ahead, afraid of looking at Tamara in case everyone could read his thoughts.

'You're running in the morning?' Annoyance slapped at him from the woman beside him.

'A ten k run on the North Shore.' It had never occurred to him to mention it.

Michael asked, 'What about you, Tamara?'

'I'm not running anywhere.'

'So you'll be there for drinks.' Michael laughed.

'Sorry, but I can't make it either.' She sounded as if she'd like to cancel their appointment.

'You both going to the same thing, by any chance?' asked one of the older nurses with a hint of laughter in her voice.

He looked at Tamara. *Shall we tell them?*

She glared at him, then just as abruptly sighed and lifted her head a notch to nod. 'I guess.'

Reaching for her hand, Conor gave it a little squeeze. He'd had a reprieve and from now on would try harder to include her in everything. 'Go on.'

Best Tamara told them. She had expressed doubts over this only last night when they'd talked on the phone, but if she was ready then she needed to put it out there, let go of some of the things holding her back.

Her fingers returned his squeeze. 'We're going to see a midwife and then I'm having a scan.'

Delighted gasps echoed around the department. Hugs ensued.

'Congratulations.' Michael shook his hand. 'You still should join us afterwards. We can have a double celebration.'

Not sure how Tam would feel about that.

'We'll be there,' she told Michael quickly.

Giving him a taste of his own medicine by not consulting with him before accepting? 'Seems that's a yes. Might as well have a meal at the same time.'

Tamara tugged her hand away and picked up a file from the counter, like she was dismissing him. Regretting that they'd told everyone? Or still assimilating the fact they weren't alone with this any more? Tam would struggle with having shared something so personal.

He leaned in to say, for her ears only, 'Yesterday I over-heard two nurses commenting on your tiredness and how you're not eating as much as usual. By telling everyone, we've stopped the gossip before it gets out of hand.'

Troubled eyes met his gaze. 'Or started something big-ger.'

The media. The ever-present monster. Maybe she'd been right to think it best to hide the fact she was pregnant. But that wouldn't work. Babies tended to become very obvious after a few months of incubating. 'Hey, guys, one more thing.' Probably huffing into the wind, but worth a try. 'We'd prefer it if our news could stay among the team, and not be broadcast over the city.'

'Fair enough.'

'Good idea.'

'Of course.'

They'd have to wait to know if everyone was completely with them on this. Or go to Sydney sooner rather than later.

The phone from Ambulance Headquarters rang and ended the chattering.

But not the questions buzzing in Conor's head as he picked up a patient's notes. Did he even want to move to Sydney now that the reason for going had disappeared? Would Tam be just as comfortable in Dublin? Or should they stay here and brazen it out? No. Not that. It would be unfair on the baby, and Tam.

Spring air floated before him. Soft fingers alighted on his forearm. 'Conor? Thanks.'

'What'd I do?'

'Made me see how much of a secret I've been living. I don't tell people, friends even, much about what I'm up to and that's been stifling. For the last two years I've been in shut-down mode. Not the way I used to live and...' she drew a breath and lifted her shoulders '...not how I intend bringing up my child.' Her eyes were filled with surprise and something else. Relief.

To hell with being at work. Conor leapt to his feet and wrapped an arm around her shoulders, placed a soft kiss on her forehead. Okay, so not the kiss he wanted to give but, yes, they were in the middle of the emergency department. 'Go, girl. You will do just great. Never forget I've got your back.' Another sneaky kiss and he stepped back, still watching her. 'Hey, no tears, 'cos you're making my eyes well up and that is so not a good look when I'm the boss around here.'

Slipping the spring green floaty top over her head, Tamara peered into the ridiculously small mirror in the staff locker room. If that image didn't raise a smile on Conor's dial then she might as well go back to baggy tees.

Hugging herself, she laughed softly. In February she'd been walking past a shop that had once been her favourite go-to place for great clothes and had spied this blouse in the window. It had been one of those have-to-have moments that had cost far too much money even in the end-of-summer sale. Since then the blouse had languished at the back of her wardrobe. But today spring was in the air and in the colours of the blouse. Spring came filled with promise, exactly how she felt at the moment. The media wouldn't rule her life again. Neither would Peter get a look in. But Conor? Oh, yes. Bring him on, centre stage. And... Tamara did a little dance on the spot. And she was going to meet her baby in a little over an hour.

The door swung wide and Kelli strolled in. 'Hello? Has anyone seen my friend? The one who hides in frumpy clothes and doesn't wear make-up? The one who doesn't own gorgeous, to-die-for blouses and tight capris. Seems you haven't forgotten how make-up works either.'

'I saw that woman leaving home early this morning,' Tamara gave straight back. 'You're stuck with me now.'

'I'm not even going to ask.'

Wait two minutes and I bet you do. I'll save you the bother.

'It's time, Kelli.'

Her friend nodded. 'I agree.'

'Way past it, if I'm honest. This baby's shaking me up something terrible. But it's also exciting. I want to do right by him or her, which means moving on, dropping the past.'

'Nothing to do with Conor, then? You're not trying to impress him?' A cheeky grin took any edge out of her words. 'Because you need to know baby has no idea what you're wearing, but Conor is going to melt on the spot when he sees you.'

Tamara smiled. 'Ninety percent to do with him. I've been a fashion nightmare far too long. It's surprising Conor took me to bed in the first place, don't you think?'

'No, I don't. You've always been more than your clothes, girlfriend. But I'm thrilled to see you all dressed up and looking like you own the world.'

'I'll pay you when I've been to the cash machine.' The excitement bubbled up again. Today she'd made inroads into getting on with this new life that made her feel proud. Strong, even. Stronger.

'I can't wait to hear about the scan. You will tell me everything, won't you?'

'I'll bore you to sleep with the details. Oh, Kells, it's true. I'm having a baby.' A little life was growing inside her and she was about to hear its heart beating and see it moving. A lone tear sneaked out from the corner of her eye.

'Yeah, you are.' A hint of wistfulness came through those three words.

'Kelli?'

'If you need a godmother for this baby, you've got my number.'

'The job's yours, as of now.' It was something she'd already decided on, had just been waiting to discuss it with Conor first. Oops. She needed to rectify that fast.

The stunned look on Conor's face when she walked into his office raised her self-awareness to a whole new level and made her realise how low she'd gone. 'I thought you looked beautiful before.' He came around his desk to kiss her. 'I had no idea.'

'Are you ready?' Time was moving too fast. 'Rush hour's started and I'd hate to be late for this appointment.'

He swung his car keys from his fingers. 'We're off.'

'Snails are passing us,' she muttered as the line of traffic stalled at lights for the umpteenth time.

'School's out. It's to be expected.'

'You're too calm.'

'One of us has to be.' Conor lifted her hand from her lap and kissed each finger in turn.

'Aren't you tearing apart with excitement? With the need to see our baby?' Her stomach was going to take days to recover from this, churning away like a washing machine stuck on fast.

'Oh, yeah.'

The car jerked forward, stopping an inch from the car in front. 'Come on, move,' Tamara yelled, and pounded her knees with her fists. 'This is ridiculous.' She turned on Conor. 'You can stop laughing and all.'

'We have forty minutes to cover less than a kilometre. I don't see the problem.'

Leaning back, she closed her eyes and counted to ten. 'Why are men so damned reasonable?' Opening her eyes, she fixed him with a glare. 'Or is it only you?'

He just laughed. Again.

'You are excited.' Yes. 'We're on the same page.'

'Better get used to it.' He grinned. 'This is how it should be for evermore.'

Her happiness tripped. Righted itself. She'd run with his easy talk. New day, new outlook. 'Um, just one thing. I was going to talk to you first but the words kind of slipped out. I told Kelli I'd like her to be baby's godmother.'

'That's fine. She's a perfect choice.'

'You agree as easily as that?' Unbelievable. 'Even if we leave the country?'

'Yep. Gives me leeway for my stuff-ups.' Conor was tapping out a tune on the steering wheel as he waited for the lights to change. On the footpath two youngsters sped past on skateboards. 'Kids, eh? I can't believe we're going to see our child. *Ours*.'

'If we ever get there.'

'Is it a boy or a girl?'

'Does that matter?' She didn't mind one way or the other, though she had started calling the baby he or him. Probably because of the mental images her mind drew up on a regular basis of a much younger version of Conor. That black hair; those blue eyes that were more often than not filled with warmth and laughter; the smile to beat all smiles that turned her to putty.

Beside her Conor laughed. 'Not at all, but I want to know so I can call the baby her or him and be right. I want all the things I plan for our child to be in the right colour, the right head space, the right shape.'

'You want pink for a girl and blue for a boy?' Tamara spluttered.

'Old-fashioned, huh?'

'Very. Believe me, I won't be buying only pink if we have a girl. There'll be every colour of the rainbow in her clothes, her room, her toys.'

'Ah, but no pink anywhere if it's a boy.'

'Deal.' Another hand squeeze. 'Though what if he wants to be a ballerina?'

'Does he have to be a pink one?'

'His call.'

'Fair enough. Pick our battles is what you're really saying.' He turned to her and placed his hands on her shoulders. 'You're awesome, you know that?'

Her mouth dried. About to shake her head, she stopped. If Conor thought that she'd take the compliment, enjoy it. Accept it. 'I think we're a great pair of would-be parents. I'll make the rules and you follow them.' She held her breath while waiting to see how he dealt with her joke.

He laughed some more. 'Sounds like something my sisters would say.'

'So I'm in with a chance with the Irish gang, then?'

'I wouldn't put you in the bonkers league but, yeah, they'll adore you.' He gave an exaggerated sigh. 'And I'll be in deeper trouble.'

Tamara stared at the image on the screen beside her. A tiny human floated before her eyes as she listened to the gentle rhythm of her baby's heart. Her chest expanded, filling with love for this child. Her child. Hers and Conor's. Blindly scrabbling around, she found Conor's hand, grabbed it and held on tight, never taking her eyes off the baby. Words were beyond her. Probably just as well. She wouldn't make any sense.

'Will you look at that?' Conor's voice sounded all clogged up as he stared at the image. Their faces were reflected back at them from the screen as their baby moved in the fluid supporting it. 'That's my baby,' he choked around some obstacle no doubt in the back of his throat.

'Our baby,' Tamara admonished in an equally starstruck tone when speech was possible. 'Isn't he beautiful?'

Now it was Conor gripping her hand tight, holding on like he couldn't take in what he was seeing. 'To think I believed I could forego becoming a parent. I didn't have a clue. It wasn't an easy decision, I admit.' His free hand waved through the air. 'I don't know what to say.'

'Different from seeing your nieces and nephews after they were born, eh?'

'Doesn't come close. To think what I wanted to do to those condom manufacturers when you said you were pregnant. Now I could kiss them.'

Tamara continued watching the small movements on the screen as the sonographer pressed the wand deeper into her belly. 'Guess you get to hear all sorts of weird and wonderful conversations while you're doing scans,' Tamara said to her.

She grinned. 'You have no idea. You two are boringly normal.'

Normal was good. For them at any rate. So far not much else had been. 'Is everything as it should be?' Tamara asked with a hitch in her voice, her throat suddenly dry.

'Yes. Baby's the right length for twelve weeks. The heart rate is good.'

Tamara relaxed. 'That's the best news so far.'

'Do you want to know the baby's gender?'

'I do,' Tam answered quickly, then looked at Conor. 'Do you?'

'Absolutely,' Conor agreed. 'We can't keep calling the baby he or him without knowing for sure there's a wee lad in there.'

'You're just thinking of the paint pails.'

The sonographer rolled the wand across Tamara's stomach, staring at the screen as she found the view of the baby she required. 'There you go. You're having a boy.'

Wonder ripped through Tamara. A boy. Not he or it, but a boy. For real.

'A son.' Wonder deepened Conor's accent. 'Not that it would've mattered if we were having a girl.'

'An All Black in the making.' Except their son probably wouldn't be growing up in New Zealand. 'A soccer player or a rally driver.'

'Not a ballerina, then?' Conor grinned. Then he shivered and the excitement went out in his eyes, the colour faded from his face.

Tamara focused entirely on the man who was changing her life for the better. 'Conor?' Her hand gripped his tightly. She shook him when he wouldn't meet her gaze. 'Look at me.'

He shuddered.

Then she knew. He was afraid for his son. Leaning closer, she spoke quietly. 'Forewarned is forearmed, remember?' She turned to the sonographer now cleaning her gear. 'Could we have a few moments to ourselves, please?'

'Not a problem. I'll print some images for you and then the room is all yours.'

Tamara waited impatiently. Yes, she wanted those pictures. But right this moment she needed to talk to Conor, to help him past his fear. This time she had to be the strong one, had to ignore her own worries about baby's heart. For now anyway.

The door hadn't closed behind the technician when Tamara lifted Conor's cold hand to her lips and placed a kiss on each knuckle. 'You have every right to worry, Conor, but do you really want to spend the coming years going around in a cloud of doom and gloom when you could be enjoying so many things with your son?'

'A son whose life might be taken in an instant.'

'A son who will most likely annoy the hell out of you as he grows up and who will give you equally as much pleasure and joy and pride.'

'How can you believe that without being terrified something will go wrong?'

'I have to. I can't let fear dictate, otherwise our son's life will be a misery. I've lived that life recently, and it's a waste of valuable time. A complete waste.'

Winter was in the blue eyes that connected with hers. 'I wish I had half your strength.'

'You do.'

His eyes widened. 'I panic.'

'Sure you do. I go crazy if I see a spider. Not in the same league, but in the end just as pointless and just as uncontrollable.' As had been Peter. It wouldn't have mattered if she'd not done as he'd bidden, he'd have found a way to steal everything from her and her parents.

The tip of Conor's tongue slid along his lips. 'You're good for me, you know that?'

'Keep believing that and we'll get along fine.' She was learning to accept how good Conor was for her too. They were making progress.

CHAPTER NINE

'WANT TO GO to the mall in the morning?' Conor heard Kelli ask Tamara over the noise of their work friends at the pub. 'The shops are filled with new summer styles.'

He stared into his water glass as he waited for her reply. Not that he'd asked Tamara to do anything over the weekend yet. He'd been leaving that until they were alone. If they got to be alone tonight. Celebrating Michael's birthday and then the news about their baby had become a long haul even when drinking nothing more innocuous than water in deference to tomorrow's race. The night was taking its toll on Tamara. She looked exhausted, but also the happiest he'd seen her in a long time. If not ever.

'I thought I'd go and watch Conor run his race in the morning.'

'Are you serious?' Conor asked without thought.

'You don't want me there?' Tamara asked around that smile that hadn't slipped once since leaving Auckland Radiation Services.

And before it did he answered, 'It's more than all right, but be warned, you'll be bored most of the time.'

'I can stand with other bored onlookers.' That smile grew, filled with warmth and something else. Something more than affection? For him?

Hard to know. Tamara hid her feelings well. Like he

did. But then he didn't know his feelings for her. Couldn't fathom them, knew he wanted to be with her always, but did that mean he loved her? There was this lurking sensation in his gut that once he admitted he might, she'd sense his change and withdraw when he'd only just got her onside. Plenty of time to think about this. 'You'd prefer that to a mall filled with shops and sales? You're nuts.'

'I get to spend time with you, don't I?' The smile softened further.

'I know when I'm not wanted.' Kelli rolled her eyes and headed to the bar.

'Something's up with her.' Tamara's eyes tracked her friend.

'Go with her tomorrow if you're worried.'

'As much as I'd like to, you and I have a lot to work through and for baby's sake that's more important at the moment.' Her hand lay on her tummy while her gaze was still on her friend. 'I'll see Kelli during the week. It's her grandfather's birthday on Sunday and I know everyone's worried about his health.'

'But you think there's something else?'

'It was the sadness in her eyes when I told her about our baby. Like she believes she'll never have the same opportunity.'

Conor leaned close, and kissed the corner of her mouth. 'You know what that's like.' Another kiss. 'And look how it's turned out for you.'

Tamara snuggled into him. 'Pretty darned good, huh, Dr Maguire?'

'More than,' he agreed. 'I want you to meet someone tomorrow.'

Sitting up, she locked her eyes on him. 'Who?'

'My mam. Thought we could have a call. I'd have to check she's at home, otherwise we'll try on Sunday. But be warned, Sunday means the whole tribe will probably turn up at her house.'

He could see doubt warring with pleasure in her face. 'Is this to tell her about the baby?'

'Yes. She'll be thrilled.'

'But you're not married. Will that be okay?' Her voice trailed off.

Now was not the time to talk about marriage—not in a pub with too many sets of ears flapping. 'Mam will be more than happy we're having a baby. Trust me on this.'

'I wish my mother would listen long enough to hear my news.'

'Want to try again over the weekend?'

'I can, but I guarantee the result will be the same.' Now that smile had disappeared completely, tugging at his heartstrings.

He wanted to smother this woman with love and affection, give her all the things she'd missed out on for so long. There was that L word again. What was going on in his head? Patience. His new go-to word. Rushing either him or Tam was not the way to do things. 'Want another sparkling water? Or shall we head home?'

Her eyes widened. 'Home? Whose?'

As in we don't live together. Yep, he got it. 'My apartment's closer.' *And not filled with objects from your past.*

'I have nothing but the best memories of your apartment.' Her smile was slow, and teasing, and struck him right under his ribs.

'Up to making more?'

Tam stood and held her hand out to him. 'Show me.'

Memories. Tamara hugged herself as she waited at the finish line the next day for Conor to appear around the far corner. They'd made some amazing ones last night back at Conor's place. She was stacking up a load lately. All with one central figure.

Conor.

There. Running hard as he aimed for the end of the race, strangers and her cheering him on. His jaw was fixed in a determined way she'd not seen before. Those long athletic legs stretching out, eating up the metres, his strong arms pumping the air. Doing this to keep healthy, to stay alive. She could only hope he didn't go crazy and overdo the fitness thing now that he was becoming a father. Too much could be as dangerous as too little.

'Go, Conor,' she yelled, and jumped up and down. 'You can do it.'

He wasn't about to win the race—someone had already done that. He wasn't even in the first couple of hundred runners home, but he obviously wanted to keep the place he had, and therefore so did she.

As he passed her she waved and shouted, 'You're amazing, Conor Maguire.' She couldn't run one kilometre, let alone ten, in a good time.

His running shorts and singlet clung to his sweat-drenched skin, outlining every muscle, the wide chest and narrow hips she adored exploring. Not the perfect athlete's body, but perfect to her. The body that fitted hers, made hers hum. The man who was determined to be a part of her and their baby's life regardless of any argument she might put up. The man she wanted onside every step of the way with their child. With her. For life.

Memories. Those new ones felt good, right.

She walked towards him. He'd finished, was leaning over, hands on his knees as he took in great lungsful of air. She touched his shoulder, then his head. 'You're nuts. You know that, don't you?'

His eyes were that light blue she adored when he dragged his head up. 'I figured out halfway through that it would've been as energetic to have stayed in bed with you this morning, and a lot more enjoyable.'

'Good answer.' She dug into the day pack she'd carried slung over her shoulder all morning and pulled out his towel and water bottle. 'Here.'

'I was a bit short on energy today.' He grinned.

'That'll teach you for carrying that rubbish bin out to the roadside this morning.'

'Nothing to do with the midnight antics in my bedroom, you reckon?'

She stepped back, hands up. 'I'm not taking the blame for your poor performance. In the race, I mean,' she added with a laugh.

'Is that a compliment? Wonders will never cease.' He shrugged out of the singlet and pulled on a sweatshirt. 'Let's get out of here.'

'You don't want to stay for the speeches and prizegiving?' Not something that would excite her, but she hadn't been the one to put all the effort into running for the children's charity.

Conor shook his head. 'I'd prefer a shower, cold beer and food, and time with you—alone.'

Tenderness spread throughout her. This special treatment was—well, special. She was so not used to it. What if—? No. Conor meant what he'd said, showed her in actions as much as he put it in words. He cared. There was a soft tightening behind her breasts as she slipped her hand into his. 'Let's go.'

She was getting used to being this close to him. She felt safe. But her heart was still secure despite that achy nudge. The love factor was still on lock-down.

Tamara grabbed her phone to see who was calling. The band tightening around her heart relaxed. 'Morning, Conor.'

She'd missed him from the moment he'd climbed out of her bed midevening last night to go back to his apartment. At her insistence. They'd spent the afternoon doing weekend chores, grocery shopping for each of them, going to the farmers' market, doing their laundry, and getting on too well. Spooked at how well, Tamara had suggested Conor go back to his place after they'd made love. It was one thing to acknowledge to herself she was happy with the way they were progressing; it was quite another to be reminded of it at every turn, each glance. Too much too soon. She just wasn't as ready to have Conor full time in her day-to-day life as she'd thought.

'Hey, Tam, how are you?'

Back to calling her Tam. He can't have been too peeved at being kicked out of her bed. 'Couldn't be better.' Or was he using that to wind her in as he wished?

Stop it, Tamara Washington. Give the guy a break. He deserves so much better of you than this.

'What about you?'

'Bursting with energy.'

'After that ten k. Impressive.'

'You forgot to add the rest of my activities.' There was laughter in his voice. Was Conor happy? With her? To be with her?

'I haven't forgotten anything.' Scary. What really got to her was that it mattered. Conor in her life outside work was beginning to mean something special.

'Feel like catching the ferry across to Devonport for lunch? The day's perfect for being out on the water.'

'That'd be awesome.' The sky was blue for as far as she could see from her window. 'The harbour should be calm enough for my stomach.' It had done its morning ritual hours ago.

'You worry too much,' he admonished softly, that

brogue tickling her in places best left alone unless he was standing right beside her. 'You're usually back to normal in no time at all.'

'What don't you notice?'

'Hard not to when you're usually scoffing a pastry by nine o'clock.'

'Stop talking and get around here.' She pressed 'off', feeling a hundred percent happier than before he'd phoned. So simple. One short call and her life was back on track. The new track that involved Conor and the baby and a life.

The one that had had her going through her wardrobe earlier to throw out all the shapeless clothes she'd accumulated. How had she let herself get so down that she hadn't cared about her looks? No one from her past would believe that. Right from when she'd been a toddler, clothes had been as important as being her father's special girl.

Today she sported another pair of capri pants and a blouse from a time when she had dressed well, the surprise being that they still fitted perfectly. But not for long. Her fingers splayed across her stomach. Did maternity wear come with style and flair? Must do, surely?

'I'm going on a date,' she sang as she applied eyeliner. A real dinky-die date with a real dinky-die hot man with a body dreams were made of.

Look what usually happened to her dreams.

She shivered, slapped the eyeliner pencil on the counter and tugged the mascara wand out of its tube.

Not the way to go, Tamara.

Ding-dong.

'Coming,' she sang. Since Conor's first visit here, on the day she'd told him she was pregnant, she'd grown to love the sound of her doorbell.

Even better was the kiss Conor gave her the moment she opened the door. His mouth claimed hers as though he would never leave her again. When he pushed his tongue across her lips she opened her mouth and let him in. Savoured his taste, the feel of him, his scent. Truly knew him, not as the father of her baby, the man she'd worked with for nearly a year, the guy who had sworn to stand by her, but as Conor Maguire—the whole package, the man who she could too easily fall in love with if she ever relaxed enough. Her body ached for him from her toes to her mouth. 'Have we got time?' she whispered through their kiss.

She was swung up against Conor's chest and carried towards her bedroom without his mouth shifting off hers. Guess that was a yes, then.

Some time later Conor stepped out of the bathroom, saying, 'Let's go and have us some fun. Have you got a jacket? There could be a sea breeze while we're on the ferry.'

Tamara snatched up the one she'd put on the table earlier. 'Yes, and sunscreen to protect my pasty winter skin.'

'It's me who'll need that. My Irish skin can't handle the Kiwi sun.'

The crossing was calm. Baby stomach hadn't objected. Bathed in sunshine, Devonport was busy with city dwellers out for a stroll and an alfresco lunch.

Walking slowly, her hand in Conor's, stopping to window-gaze at pottery, art and clothes, Tamara hadn't felt so relaxed in years. 'It's as though everything's coming together perfectly,' she spilled as they sat down at a small round table outside a lunch bar. Then the familiar dread crept in. Too perfectly. 'I shouldn't have said that.'

'Think you're tempting fate?' Conor asked.

'Over the last couple of years, whenever I've dared to think things might be looking up, something awful has happened.' And since they'd never looked up half as much as they were now, she might have a lot to fear.

'You're not on your own any more. We're a team. We're going to watch out for each other.'

'Aw, shucks. You say the loveliest of things sometimes.' *Sniff, sniff.*

'I wouldn't if I knew it was going to make you cry.' With the paper napkin from the plate at his elbow he gently dabbed her eyes.

Which only increased the volume of water oozing down her cheeks.

'Hey, steady. These napkins aren't made for waterfalls.' Conor's lips tipped upwards, sending her stomach into a riot of butterflies.

'I wish my dad could've met you. He'd have liked you.' Dad had dreamed of walking his daughter down the aisle since the first time he'd held her in his hands. Which had absolutely nothing to do with Conor. She wasn't marrying him, just setting up house to provide for their child.

'I'd have liked that too.' Conor screwed up the wet napkin and dropped it in the centre of the table. 'Want to order?'

They shared a large Hawaiian pizza and Conor had a beer while Tamara stuck to water. Leaning back in her chair, she glanced along the road to where the tide lapped at the edge of the promenade. 'I could stay here for ever.' There wasn't a driving need to fill gaps in conversation or to wonder what Conor might be thinking. 'Have you decided about following up on the Sydney interview?'

'How would you feel if I did? Would you be okay with joining me there? If you are and I get the position then I'll stay a few extra days to look for somewhere for us to live.' Caution lay between them, the cosy atmosphere gone.

'There's nothing to keep me here apart from my job, which I was going to give up at the end of the year to go to university. Kelli is my only friend and she would be the last person to want me not getting on with my life, and that's with you now. You and wee man.' Her hand circled her belly. Was it her imagination or had her stomach begun to pop out now that she'd accepted her pregnancy?

'You aren't agreeing to move just to keep me happy?'

'Not at all. I'm all for making changes in my life, and there are a lot coming up. Why not start our new life in a place neither of us has been before?'

'That job in Sydney's only for twelve months and then we get to repeat this conversation.'

'Done. Sydney it is. Because I know you'll be offered the position. They'd have to be crazy not to.' Something like excitement fizzed in her veins. 'I feel I'm starting to live again. My primary goal is no longer to keep my head down and avoid facing up to difficult people or decisions.'

'You were focused on going to university and med school.'

'I procrastinated for ever. All those "t"s and "i"s. If you hadn't kept telling me I could do anything if I wanted it badly enough, I'd probably still be dithering about applying.' Now the decision had been taken away from her it was surprising how little that hurt. How could it when she was going to become a mother?

'You could apply in Sydney.'

He'd just said he'd only be there a year. Anyway, 'I don't want to become a doctor at the moment. Being a hands-on mum is what I'd like to be next. Does that make me sound flaky? Unreliable?' She didn't wait for an answer. He might say yes. 'Imagine all those hours I'd have to spend studying and later working and there'd be a wee man at home not getting my full attention. I don't think so. I'll get a part-time job nursing.'

'You can stay at home if you want. Be a full-time mother.'

'We'll see.' It was too early to accept his offer, if she could ever bring herself to do that. She was still getting her head around the fact she had agreed to leave Auckland. It felt right, but it was a huge leap in trust. What a difference a week made, unless she was back to her old tricks and handing over her heart too easily.

No, I refuse to believe that.

Until proved wrong, I will believe in Conor. Totally.

Because otherwise she'd do her head in, working it all out. Anyway, her heart still belonged to her, not Conor.

'We don't have to hurry back to the city.' Conor watched Tam across the table. 'Want to walk along the beach?' A relaxed Tamara was something to enjoy. She didn't do it often enough. Was he about to push too hard, too fast?

'That's a great idea.'

Placing some money under his plate, Conor rose and reached for her hand. 'I've never held a woman's hand so often.' He winced. 'Sorry, that wasn't exactly tactful.'

'We come with pasts. Not that I know anything about yours. Come on, spill. Any world-stopping affairs? Or a great love of your life that didn't work out?'

Now who was being tactless? But he rolled with it because it might help his cause by knocking down some more barriers. 'There was a girl I thought I'd love for ever, until the day she swiped my piece of birthday cake from my school bag and left me her mouldy scone. We were seven.'

'Silly girl. She might've got the whole cake if she'd played nice.'

He nudged her. 'Remember that.' He swung their hands between them. 'Next I fell hard for a student at med school until she turned up one day sporting a rock on her finger and her resignation in the other hand. She'd found the specialist she wanted to marry and live the good life with.'

'That must've hurt.'

'Only my pride. We weren't well suited. For a while I stuck to having fun without commitment, the only way to go when most hours were taken up with study.' The old demon rose. 'After my heart attack there was no way I was looking for a serious relationship.'

Her fingers jerked in his, but she didn't withdraw.

Conor stopped and took her into his arms to gaze into those deep eyes. 'Seems from the day I met you life took a bat and beat me over the skull, because everything I adhered to regarding relationships flew out the window. It has taken time for me to recognise what was going on.' Did she see where he was headed?

Her tongue worried at the centre of her top lip. 'You're okay with that? It's been a shock for both of us.'

'I'm not just talking about the baby, Tam.'

'Oh.' Worry, worry. Then she pulled away and continued walking along the beach.

They were still surrounded by kids and dogs, and couples, and elderly women chatting. Conor went with Tam, ready to wait a bit longer, despite the impatience sizzling in his veins.

Her fingers slipped into his again. 'That heart attack has a lot to answer for.'

'Yeah.' Too much. But not all bad. 'My mother struggled to come to terms with losing Dad and my brother. There was a while there when occasionally she'd go out to the store to get something and not come home.'

Tam gasped. 'Where were you?'

'The first time I was with a playmate and his mother went to find her. The second time it happened during the night and I woke up. My crying must've been loud because the neighbour rang the cops, who turned up real fast.'

'Were you taken away?'

'Fortunately, no. There's only so much a four-year-old could cope with.' That would've meant the start of welfare and strangers and he had already been broken-hearted. 'One of the cops was Dave and he'd known Mam for a long time so he stayed with me while his colleagues searched for her. It was Dave who spent hours with Mam, talking about whatever was important to her, and after that whenever she felt the urge to get away she'd ring him.'

'Is this the man who became your stepfather?' Warm brown eyes were turned on him.

'The one and only. If I couldn't have my dad, then he was the next best option. Not once did I feel different or not a part of the family that was to come.' He'd got lucky. Twice. 'I was better off than some kids at school who had their real fathers.'

'I'm glad. Guess that's why you're determined to be there for our young man.' Tamara stretched up to kiss him.

A gentle, sweet kiss that set his heart racing. They were at the end of the promenade. Alone apart from one dog and a sky full of screeching seagulls.

With his hands on her shoulders he held her gently. 'Not the only reason.' His stomach lurched. *Too fast, man.* But waiting wasn't an option. There was so much to sort out and not a lot of time. 'Tam, will you marry me?'

Just as well his hands were holding her shoulders. He got the feeling she'd have dropped in a heap otherwise.

She was staring at him. 'Did you just propose? To *me*?'

Ouch. Not rushing to accept, then. 'Yes, Tam, you. I want to marry *you*. For us, and for our child.'

'For us?' The words were strangled.

He nodded as he smiled away his worry and gave her reassurance. 'Yes, us. We've practically agreed to live together, to raise our child jointly, to move around the world as a couple. Marriage would be the icing on the cake.'

Her shoulders sagged into his hands. Her mouth dropped. 'Oh.'

'I care about you, Tam. A lot. I want this. A family, you.' Conor spilled out the words in a rush of honesty. 'You've got under my skin and I can't ignore you. You make me hope for more, and believe anything's possible. I think we can have a wonderful future together.'

Her eyes widened and she straightened. 'Truly?' Doubt lurked on her mouth, in her face.

'This is not something I'd make up.' He wasn't her ex. He had no hidden agenda. He needed to remember that, and give her time. 'All I want is to make you happy. That'll make me happy too.'

'You care for me that much?' Her acceptance was sinking in. It was there in the softening of her mouth, the colour turning her cheeks pink, her hands spreading across his chest.

'Absolutely.' Was he falling in love with Tam? Yep, he could be. 'I don't want you thinking I'm out to hurt you in some way. I'd never do that.'

'You don't think you're rushing things? It's only been a week since we found out we're joined together for ever by a baby.' She was stalling. Listening to her heart *and* her head?

'I tend to make up my mind and act on it immediately. But I can say that from that first night together you've been residing in my mind, taunting me, distracting me, making me sleep-deprived, and it has taken learning about baby to tease that wide open. That, and hearing about your past and why you are who you are.'

'That was important?'

'Absolutely. I like to understand what makes people tick, and with you it was becoming a full-time need. I could see you hurting at times, and how you hid a lot from everyone by putting up insurmountable barriers, and yet you came to me so willingly that night.' Conor's thumbs caressed her shoulders. 'I take that as a compliment.'

Her face softened as she studied him. 'Yes. Let's get married.' She blinked, stared at him. She hadn't thought this through. She'd be thinking she'd made the same rash decision as she had with her ex.

'Tamara?' He shook her gently, his heart heavy, knowing she needed space. 'You're sure? If you want a few days to think about it I'll understand.'

'You haven't spun false hope around me to suck me in. I don't want to live on the edge of something I might have, never knowing if I will actually get it or not. I need honesty and reality.' Rising up onto her toes, she whispered, 'This isn't how I envisioned accepting a proposal, but I will marry you, Conor Maguire.' And then she sealed her words with a kiss like no other she'd given him. It was full of hunger, and longing, and commitment, and caution.

He didn't recognise love in the mix.

Patience, man, patience. He hadn't exactly been brimming with love either. That was still working its way into his psyche, and could turn around and disappear before reaching its full potential. Those old gremlins were still in charge.

Conor was the one to break away, his chest rising and falling as he breathed fast, feeling out of sorts and not sure where they were headed. Other than bed some time later. 'What is it about you that turns me into a raging sex maniac? If we were anywhere but on a public beach with half of the city wandering past, I'd have you naked so fast it would be crazy.'

Tamara was swaying on her feet, and he caught her to him. She croaked in a heat-hazed voice, 'Let's go home. We're not crazy, not at all.'

But maybe they were. Nearly having sex on the promenade. Agreeing to marry with no lead-in time and no declarations of love. Having a baby after one night together. What the heck? Might as well go for broke. 'Tomorrow after work we'll visit a jeweller's shop so you can choose an engagement ring.'

'No.' Tamara whipped around to stare at him. 'Sorry, but I don't want an engagement ring.'

His mouth soured. She'd changed her mind already. Shortest engagement on the planet. 'Not now? Or not at all?'

'I didn't put that very well. What I mean is all I'd like is a wedding ring. A solid band with maybe one stone. A sapphire or ruby. Not a blazing big diamond.' She shuddered. 'I want this to be about you and me. We're not flashy, or false. We care about each other, about our baby. We're starting our joint life. You and me,' she repeated. Her eyes were pleading with him to understand.

'Got it in one.' He swung her up in his arms and held her close to kiss her. Got it in one. 'You and me and our son.'

CHAPTER TEN

TAMARA FOLDED THE dishcloth and hung it on the door of Conor's oven. 'Done.'

'Then it's time to call Mam and give her the good news.'

Her heart gave one hard kick. It had to happen, but tonight? When she was still getting her head around being engaged to Conor? Telling other people would make it more real.

It is real.

She swallowed down on her apprehension. 'Will anyone else be there?' Any one of those sisters he obviously adored.

'It's a family tradition to have brunch at Mam and Dave's house if you're anywhere near Dublin on Sundays. At least one of my sisters and her brood will be there.'

'Will your mother be happy about you marrying a Kiwi?' Nerves cranked up. Conor's mother might think she'd keep her son from returning to Ireland permanently.

'Why ever not? I suspect she might've been hoping I would meet someone while I was away.'

'That's okay, then.' She wished. And picked up the photo frame with the image of their baby in it. Her finger skimmed over the glass while her heart knocked on her ribs.

'Tam, I'd like you to talk to her. Everyone there for brunch will be lining up to say hello.'

She pushed her chin forward. Might as well leap in and get it over. 'Sure.'

'Get used to it. You're about to become part of a large, whacky family. They'll have a load of questions for us.' He laughed. 'Not that any one of them will wait for an answer before going on to the next question.'

'You look happy when you're talking about them. Have you ever been homesick since leaving Ireland?'

'I've had massive bouts at times, but I haven't been ready to hop on a plane and head home. The reason I left was still there.' Conor kissed her on the nose. 'You've turned my life around and now I'm ready for anything.'

Including marrying her. Was he certain about that? Or would he rethink his proposal when he'd had time to contemplate all the ramifications? Tamara returned the kiss, but on his stubbly chin, and then bit down on the flick of desire heating her low down. 'About all those questions...'

'The ones we don't have answers for yet? Don't worry. I'll tell everyone to stop being nosy and that we'll get back to them.'

But she did worry. 'They'll listen?'

Conor shrugged. 'Not at all.' He opened his laptop, booted it up. 'That's family for you. They know no boundaries.'

A knot of anxiety formed. 'We'll tell your family, but I'd like to keep our engagement from everyone else for a bit longer.' Everything was happening too fast, rushing at her from all directions. 'I need to take a breath, get used to being with you, our baby, getting married, possibly moving to Sydney. There'll be so many questions and...' she lifted her hands in the air '...I don't have all the answers.'

'And you can't function properly without answers. Fair enough. Your wish is my command.' He said it all through a gut-tightening, desire-expanding smile.

She threw herself against him. 'Thank you,' she murmured before kissing him, deep and hard.

'What for?' Conor grinned when he came up for air.

'Being you.' She smiled back before leaning in for another searing kiss.

The laptop needed rebooting by the time they were ready to make the connection with Dublin.

'Junior here...' Conor's hand splayed across her tummy '...will turn up thinking it normal to do lots of exercise at odd hours of the day and night.'

Tamara chuckled as she spread her hand on top of Conor's much larger one. 'We do give him plenty of workouts.'

Conor tapped the internet icon. 'Let's do this.'

Oh, boy. She parked her butt on a stool, fidgeted with the bracelet on her wrist. Not ready. So not ready. Was she rushing into this without checking out everything about Conor? But, then, how did she do that? And did she really want to? It seemed underhand. But last time she'd trusted a man she'd cared for deeply she'd overlooked so many signs.

'Hey, Mam, how are you?' Happiness radiated out of Conor's eyes as he talked to his mother for a few minutes. Then he shifted the laptop so she was in the picture too. 'I've got someone I want you to meet.'

A gazillion faces appeared before her, each person pushing someone else out of the way. The cacophony of excited, almost incomprehensible Irish voices was deafening and reminded Tamara of a visit to a bird sanctuary in Queensland many years ago. How did anyone in this family know what was going on when they were all talking at once?

Conor reached for her hand, held it firmly. 'Tamara is my fiancée.'

Her mouth fell open. Not going for a slow lead-in, then. 'Ah, um, hi, everyone.'

'Hello, Tamara. You look gorgeous.'

'What do you see in our lump of a brother?'

'Hey, Tamara, are you a Kiwi?'

'Conor,' his mother shrieked. 'How long have you been seeing her and not told me?'

He leaned close to Tamara and whispered, 'See? Another reason why I came Down Under.'

She shook her head at him. 'You have no idea how fortunate you are.' How could he have left Ireland? His family? She'd never have been able to do it.

'You're not saying much,' someone, female, said.

'I'm surprised any of you can hear a thing,' she quipped.

'Meet the family,' Conor's mum responded. 'It's like this all the time.'

Conor held his hand up. 'Okay, guys, shut up for a moment. Tamara and I have things to discuss with you and I only want to say them once.' Instant silence descended.

'Unbelievable.' Tamara smiled.

'Yep,' he mouthed in her direction, before leaping right in with the next load of news. 'We're having a baby in six months. We're also probably moving to Sydney.'

Conor continued yabbering to his family, and the level of voices coming back at him was rising fast. Back to normal, Maguire style. Warmth trickled through her. By carrying Conor's baby she'd become a part of this family. So far they hadn't pulled faces or called her names. It had never ceased to shock her how someone who only recognised her from camera shots or headlines in the paper could come up and talk to her as though she was known to them. Worse, they often had plenty of advice for her, from how to get back on her feet to what she should do to pay back all those millions Peter had stolen. And now this. Amazing.

'Tamara, welcome to our family. You don't know how thrilled I am about this news. And you must call me Judy.' Conor's mother spoke directly to her. 'I guess we'd better go, but I'll talk to you again soon.'

'Th-thank y-you.' A tear sneaked down her cheek at the simple kindness shown her by a stranger. Conor's mother, until fifteen minutes ago unknown to her. Things really were looking up. With such a wonderful family, who appeared genuine, Conor must be the real deal, surely?

Leaning her head against his shoulder, Tamara ran her fingers over his chest. 'Your mother's lovely. So are Dave and all those sisters and their families.'

'You should try contacting your mother again.'

She stiffened. 'What's the point? She'll only tell me I've made yet another mistake and that I have to get on with it. Without her.'

'When did you last talk? As in really talk?'

'The day after Dad's funeral.' A lifetime ago. 'The fraud squad had just left the house with a vanload of cartons containing private papers from Dad's study.'

He started rubbing her back softly. 'You're beginning to look pregnant.' Warmth stole through her as he cupped her breast.

She placed a hand on her small baby bump. 'Mum's sister came out from Australia for Dad's funeral. She had plenty to say about me, blamed me for the fact that Mum was no longer wealthy and would have to live in relative poverty.'

'Your mother didn't disagree?'

'That's the funny thing. She did at first. Stuck up for me, saying there was no way I could've known what had been going on. She even gave me hugs and talked about Dad as we'd known him before the dementia stole his mind. It was a sad yet funny morning. We looked through photos of the three of us on holidays, at functions, doing the things families do. Of course, we had no idea what would go down later.'

'When did it all change?'

'The next morning my aunt went to town to buy some clothes. That's when the reality struck, first her and then Mum. She came storming in and threw all the photos on the floor, jumped on them and screamed at me for losing everything. She'd never qualified at anything and bemoaned Mum's luck at finding a rich man. Dad had always kept them both in funds. That day the credit cards simply didn't work any more.'

'And it was all your fault.'

'Apparently. Mum didn't want to believe my aunt so they went out and tried to buy a bracelet at the local jewellers. Same result, and the end of my relationship with my mother. She went on a rampage, visiting fashion shops to try on clothes she could no longer afford, leaving them in piles on the shop floors. It was all there in the papers that night. They flew to Australia the next day and I've never heard from Mum since. I have rung her often, only to be hung up on.'

'She cut you off when you'd done nothing more than trust the wrong man, a man her husband had believed in enough to hand over the company's operations to.' Conor tightened his hold around Tam, and she leaned into him. 'Would you want your mother to know about the baby and take part in his life if she could get past what happened?'

'Yes.' Had he lost his mind? 'Of course I want Mum to be his grandmother in more than name.' She wasn't exactly the perfect role model for a mother, but she was her mother.

'Want to try another phone call?'

'And take another king hit? No, thanks.' But she would,

just not tonight after that wonderful session talking with Conor's family.

'I've got a suggestion.'

She started to object.

'Hear me out. Write to her, tell her about us and the baby, and how we're moving to Sydney. Put it all on paper, including how you'd like her to be part of the family.'

'She'll tear it up.'

'Or she'll set it aside and keep going back to stare at the envelope with your writing on it until she can't resist it and gives in to curiosity.'

'She'll get rid of it the moment she sees my scribble.' Or would she?

'She might not. Or she might, but it would be worth the risk to get your mother back.'

A soft silence fell over them. Conor continued holding her close, and she continued soaking up the warmth he brought her. 'I'll think about it.'

Monday morning and bedlam. ED was overrun with year-three children from Parnell Primary. Parents were kept busy, trying to control the little getaways who seemed more intent on destroying the department than getting treated for bee stings.

'Tell me how so many kids were stung?' Conor shook his head at the chaos before turning back to a harassed teacher who also had stings on her arms and face. 'I've never seen anything like it.'

'Me neither. We were out on the field, playing soccer, when a swarm came up the bank and straight into our midst. It's the first time I've seen bees swarming and it was scary.'

'I bet.' He'd never experienced a swarm. 'To have all

those children out there, being attacked, would've been a nightmare.'

'I'm grateful only two had serious reactions. We did get most of the kids into the swimming pool quick smart.'

Hence all the wet clothes lying in piles around the department. Seemed most of the kids preferred being undressed than wet and cold.

Tamara approached with an amused expression lighting up her face. 'Remind me not to have more than one child, will you?' She tossed him a smile before picking up a book that had been dropped by one young patient.

Of course his gaze rested on her backside as she'd bent to retrieve the book. Of course. No problem with the chemistry between them. No difficulty with anything at this stage really. Not when he regularly felt light-headed and excited.

'How are the boys who had allergic reactions?' the teacher asked.

'One lad's doing well, but we've had to put the other on oxygen and morphine. He also reacted to the painkiller. His parents are with him, if you want to see them.'

The woman shook her head. 'They don't need me asking irritating questions. I saw them when they arrived.'

'We need to start moving some of these children out of here, preferably on their way home.' Conor glanced around the department. 'There are other patients waiting to be seen and none of these youngsters require our attention any longer.'

'Have you signed any of them out?' Tamara asked.

'Starting now.'

The teacher sighed. 'I'll get the parents together to explain that their children are ready to go.'

'That'll be a bag of laughs.' Tamara chuckled as she

watched the woman begin rounding up her charges and their families.

'We didn't need to see most of the children,' Conor mused. 'But I don't mind admitting I've enjoyed the last hour.'

'You're a natural with kids. Our wee man is so lucky to be having you as his dad,' she murmured before heading over to a group of kids objecting to picking up wet clothes.

Down, chest, down. But, hey, any compliment Tam was handing out he'd happily accept. His gaze followed her and his heart clenched as the kids laughed at something she said.

Impatience gnawed. They had everything going for them and had coped well with the king hits over the past week, and, damn it, he wanted more than he should.

'Doctor.' A parent stood in front of him.

'What can I do for you?'

'Tell me again about this EpiPen my son will always have to carry. It seems extreme when he's had bee stings before with no side effects.'

Conor nodded. 'One sting, even two or three at a time, don't always cause problems, but your lad had more than fifty today. Those would've filled his system with toxin, which will eventually disappear, but his body now recognises the toxin and even a small sting will ring warning bells and start a response you don't want to take a chance on.'

'Better to be safe than sorry?' The man nodded.

'If it was my child I'd be doing it.'

I've got a son. A son in utero, but he's real. I'm going to be a dad.

And it felt wonderful. As long as he didn't think about hearts and stoppages. Funny, but those had been far from his mind the last couple of days.

The phone buzzed at his elbow. 'Call for Dr Maguire.' It was the director of emergency services at Sydney Hospital.

'Hold on and I'll transfer this to my office.' Conor punched some buttons and raced for his room.

'Hi, there, Conor. Hope I'm not interrupting anything serious.' The director's voice boomed over the airwaves.

'Perfect timing. How's things in Sydney?' What was this call about? He'd made arrangements to fly over for the interview on Friday.

'We're having a minor heatwave. The job? That's yours. The other contender has pulled out for family reasons.'

'I'm sorry to hear that. But I'm also stoked.' He and Tam could get serious about their plans for the future. 'Thank you. I'm thrilled.'

'So are we. We'd like it if you still come over at the end of the week so we can run through your contract and get to eyeball you before you start officially.'

'Not a problem. I want to look into accommodation anyway.' He'd got the job. Conor punched the air. Another tick in the going-well stakes. Where was Tam? He couldn't wait to tell her.

'Congratulations, Dr Maguire.' Tamara lifted her glass of sparkling water in a toast the following night. 'Watch out, Sydney Hospital.'

Conor tapped his glass against hers. 'We're on our way, Tam.' He glanced around the restaurant she'd chosen to celebrate his new job. 'I can't believe how everything's falling into place so easily.'

A flicker of doubt crossed her eyes but then she smiled. 'Don't tempt fate, whatever you do.'

'That first day I walked into Auckland Central's ED and set eyes on you, I had absolutely no idea how much my life would change.' If not for Tamara's pregnancy he'd still be avoiding the things that were now making him happy.

The sweetest pink coloured her cheeks under her make-up. 'Are all Irish men so charming?'

The off-the-shoulder little black dress she wore was sensational. 'You're like another Tamara Washington. Just as beautiful and lovely with an added dose of style thrown in.'

The pink darkened to red. 'I shudder when I think how I let myself go.'

Her hand was warm under his. 'Your shapely body and stunning looks weren't all that attracted me.' The words were coming too easily for a guy not used to putting his feelings out there.

'You're embarrassing me.' Tamara toyed with her glass. 'What I wouldn't do for a glass of wine right now. There's so much to celebrate and I'm stuck with water.' Her mouth was tipping into a big smile. One that didn't quite reach her eyes.

'For the best reason.'

'Totally agree.' No doubt in her eyes now.

'Thank goodness for nights,' Tamara muttered, as she dropped her bag on the kitchen table on Wednesday and pulled open the fridge to see what to have for dinner. 'Then again maybe not.'

One soft and spongy tomato, a piece of cheese growing a healthy dose of mould—or was that unhealthy in her condition? The solitary carrot on the middle shelf was so soft she could tie a knot in it. The groceries she'd bought last weekend were still at Conor's apartment.

Thank goodness for the café at work. Another supermarket trip was imperative, but would have to wait until the weekend. Her body ached with fatigue, as though it hadn't had any sleep in a month.

Flicking the kettle on, she leaned a hip against the bench and stared out into her tiny back yard. It was as if she'd been running forward at full tilt since the day she'd told Conor she was pregnant, with no stopping to take a breath and suss everything out in a reasoned fashion. No wonder she felt as though she was slowly unravelling. The excitement of seeing her baby for the first time had gone, replaced with lethargy. Conor's proposal hadn't banished all her doubts either. In the middle of the night the old fears rose to torment her. A fast proposal so he could carry on as he'd always intended? But she had agreed to go to Sydney with him anyway. What else did he want from her?

This should be the best time of her life and yet she couldn't drag up any enthusiasm. She was so damned tired. And still uncertain of relying on her judgement.

Ding-dong.

That darned doorbell. She never had got around to taking the batteries out. But, then, she enjoyed Conor dropping in all the time. Still did, if only she could find some energy. And complete belief that he wouldn't hurt her.

Ding-dong.

'Coming,' she called. *Please be Conor.* Conor without too many questions, not Conor wanting to sort out dates for moving to Sydney, for getting married, for every damned thing.

'Hey.' He stood on the step, looking good enough to eat.

'Hey, yourself.' Pulling the door wide, she stepped back, and breathed in his man scent as he walked in. What a man. The man she wanted to trust implicitly, but couldn't quite manage to yet. Getting close, but not close enough. Following him into her kitchen, she said, 'I'm making a cup of tea. Want one?' How domestic was that, then?

'I've got a six-pack in here.'

Only then did she notice the grocery bags swinging from his hands. 'You've got more than beer there.'

'I'm on dinner. Hope you're okay with steak again?' He placed the bags on the bench and began unpacking, totally at home in her space.

'Grocery shopping was next on my to-do list. But I wasn't getting excited about it.'

'Your excitement levels have been wavering most of the week.' Conor leaned his butt against the bench and locked a formidable gaze on her. 'Are you sure everything's all right? Not having second thoughts about anything?'

Since when had Conor become challenging? Was this one of the reasons she was feeling at odds with herself? 'I'm pregnant, and that's taking everything out of me at the moment,' she snapped, more forcefully than intended.

'Sure that's not an excuse for something else?'

'Like what?'

'If I knew I wouldn't have to ask. You don't tell me much of what's going on in your head.' Frustration was building in his voice, and those hands she loved on her body were tightening their grip on his hips.

'Until last week I always dealt with problems on my own.' Usually by ignoring them or hiding. 'I am still getting used to having you on my side, in my life.'

'Problems. Are you having doubts?' Conor demanded.

'No,' she shouted, too fast and too loud. 'No,' she repeated at lower decibels. At least she didn't think so.

He continued to look at her as though searching for something. She only hoped it was something good and that he found it. Finally he returned to unpacking the shopping. 'Guess we're still on for steak, then.'

Tamara's heart cracked. They'd had their first row. A very short one, but she felt terrible. This was Conor, the father of her baby, the man who'd stepped up to his responsibilities without a blink, including asking her to marry him. The man she could be falling in love with—if only she'd relax and believe in herself. Standing behind him, she slipped her arms around his waist and laid her face between his shoulder blades. 'I'm sorry.'

Turning in her arms, Conor wrapped her into a hug. 'Me, too, Tam. Me, too.' His chin rested on her head. 'It's all taking some getting used to, isn't it?'

She nodded. 'Yeah.'

'All I ask is don't shut me out, okay?'

'Okay.' She stared at him. 'You don't think you've rushed the proposal?'

'Definitely not. It's what I want. I've never been so happy,' he said gruffly. 'I'm hoping you are too.'

'It's time I gave you a key to this place.' That would go some way to showing how much he meant to her. No one else had access to her home, not even Kelli.

'If you're sure?' A slow smile began creeping over his mouth, like a slow burn.

'Absolutely.' She trusted him with her inner sanctum. Just had to get the rest sorted out.

Conor flicked the cap off a beer. 'We haven't discussed names yet. Have you got any in mind?'

She had an idea, but hoped she wasn't opening up trouble. 'What was your brother's name?'

Whack. His hand landed on his chest. 'Sebastian.'

'And your dad's?' Might as well go for broke.

'Sebastian.'

That made it easy. As long as Conor agreed. 'Then our boy's called Sebastian.' She smiled at him, silently pleading he'd accept her idea. 'Or Sebastian Sebastian Maguire.'

The air whooshed across his lips and his eyes lit up with joy, then excess moisture swamped them and he was blinking rapidly. 'Thanks,' he managed before placing his lips on hers.

'No problem at all.' Now, that had been a lot easier than she'd expected, thinking Conor mightn't want a daily reminder of those he'd lost. She still needed to get to know him more thoroughly.

CHAPTER ELEVEN

A WOMAN'S SCREAM rent the air of the emergency department, lifting the hairs on Conor's skin. *Mam?* But of course it wasn't. Dad and Sebastian had died in another lifetime, another country.

Tamara appeared at the entrance to Resus One, gently leading a sobbing woman to a chair out of the way. She glanced across at him, her face so sad it hurt him before she refocused on the woman.

'Damn, but I love you, Tamara.'

What? His chair scraped the floor as he leapt to his feet. *I do?*

Yep, buster, you do. Lock, stock and every damned curve of her.

She couldn't have heard his whisper, but he was receiving another glance from those brown eyes and a small, intimate smile as she turned back to the patient she was with.

Conor sank back onto his chair, watching her. He'd gone and fallen in love despite doing his damnedest not to. Hard not to, considering how he couldn't get Tam out of his mind for a minute, day or night. And then she'd added a baby to the mix and bang. He was hooked.

Behind Tamara, Conor could see Michael and another emergency consultant working to resuscitate their patient, a forty-year-old man brought in after feeling unwell and noticing his mouth drooping. The man had a history of minor TIAs but today he'd hit the big mother. A stroke. And now heart failure.

Family history. It tore people apart, wrecked wonderful relationships, destroyed childhoods. Made a mockery of love. Love. He'd gone and fallen for Tamara. An oath tripped across his lips. He had made the biggest mistake of his life.

Conor needed to go help the medical team working on the stroke patient. Only then could he quieten his mind. But there were already more than enough highly skilled staff working on the guy. Instead, he tried to ignore the woman's deep, heart-wrenching sobs and began entering comments into the computer file of his last patient.

But as the woman's despair grew, there was no quietening his memories. Mam in the sitting room with two policemen. The spine-chilling screams and then the desperation in her bone-crushing hug as she'd clung to him. The tears that had lasted days. The hours when she hadn't talked, had barely known him.

The buzzer from the ambulance bay was sharp and very welcome. Now he had something solid to concentrate on, someone in need of his help who would banish these unsettling thoughts. Damned memories. To think people liked storing them up. If only they knew.

'Fractured bones at the elbow resulting in a torn artery and heavy loss of blood.' The advance paramedic handed over the patient work sheet to Conor.

A quick scan and he said to the thirty-four-year-old woman, 'I'm Conor, your doctor for the next little while. Can you tell me what happened?'

'I was painting my house and fell off the ladder.'

'Right, then let's get you into the department and find out the extent of the damage.' He took one side of the stretcher and, together with the ambulance officer, pushed his patient towards Resus Two, where Kelli and another nurse were waiting.

'On the count of three.' And they shifted the woman across to the bed.

'Need Radiology and the lab here, and Orthopaedics on the phone,' Conor ordered as he began examining the right arm, which was lying at an abnormal angle. Carefully removing the cardboard cast the ambulance crew had put in place to save extra movement and pain, he gently probed the elbow joint.

And still that woman's sobs came through loud and clear from around the corner.

Ignore her.

Conor asked his patient, 'Did you hit your head when you fell?'

'Yes, on the back, but it can't have been too hard. I didn't black out,' she wheezed through gritted teeth as pain jarred her.

'We'll get an X-ray to be doubly sure.'

Someone handed him the phone. 'Orthopaedics on the line.'

He moved away, turning his back so his words wouldn't be heard by his patient. 'I'm waiting for Radiology to come and take pictures, but I suspect a fracture to the elbow ginglymus and others to the humerus and ulna at the point of the hinge. There's heavy blood loss from a torn artery.'

'I'll be down as soon as I've put Theatre on standby,' the specialist told him.

Returning to his patient, he informed her, 'You need surgery to put that elbow back together.'

She nodded. 'Figured as much. Can someone call my husband? Let him know what's going on?'

Another family whose day had been tipped sideways.

But not as badly as the couple in the next unit. The sobs were quietening down now and Conor could hear his counterpart talking to the woman, explaining that her husband had been successfully revived.

'Until next time,' the woman cried.

Until next time. The words he'd carried around in his head since the day of his heart attack. *Until next time.* The reason for his panic attacks. That 'next time' hovered on the periphery of his mind. Most days it played nice. Occasionally, like last week, when life had been in turmoil, it had fired up, gripped his chest and sent him into a tailspin.

'Conor? This your patient?' The radiology technician had arrived.

He shook away the dark clouds in his head. 'Yes. I need as many angles as you can manage without further collateral damage.'

Conor put everything into focusing on his patient and not on the litany of doom banging around his head. But the moment the orderly wheeled her away the fears and memories were back, larger, louder than before.

He aimed for the counter and a computer to update the woman's notes. And locked eyes with Tamara as she stepped out of Resus One. Her face was drawn and that sadness in her eyes had grown heavier. His chest tightened. 'Tam?'

'We saved him, but he's got a long recovery ahead of him. His chances of walking and talking in the near future are remote.'

'How's his wife?'

'You heard her. Devastated. They've got three young boys and at the moment she's not coping. But with help she'll get there.'

That could be Tamara with Sebastian. She was saying the woman would manage but, sorry, what the hell did she know? She hadn't lost her child as the result of a heart attack. Or her husband, who'd sworn to always support her and watch her back. Yet. His hand rammed through his hair. The screams, those sobs, they'd hit him deep, dried up the happiness that'd been fizzing along his veins for nearly two weeks. Brought him back to earth. 'I've been fooling myself.'

Spinning around, he strode quickly towards his office, almost running but managing to hold himself back.

'Conor, wait for me.' From directly behind him came the one voice he did not want to hear right this minute. Not until he'd sorted his head space.

'Carry on with the patients, Tamara.' His watch read two thirty-five. Nearly home time. Well, he wouldn't be going home to stare at his four walls, but he'd be out of here fast, away from the sounds of ED, which he usually enjoyed. But not today.

'Talk to me.' She didn't give up easily.

He spun around, stabbed the air between them with his forefinger. 'No. Not now. Leave me.'

She stumbled but kept walking towards him. Shock blazed at him, but didn't slow her down. 'We're in this together, Conor. You can't walk away from me as and when it suits you.'

I can when it's for your own good.

'I can't think clearly with you talking. Give me some space, Tamara.'

Tamara. Not Tam. He could see the hurt that inflicted and briefly contemplated pausing long enough to give her a hug and tell her not to worry. But she might have every reason to worry so he refrained.

'What's this about, Conor?' That doubt she carried everywhere was wide awake and glaring at him.

'Nothing to do with you, right?' he lied, then strode

into his office and banged the door shut. Twisted the lock for good measure.

Guilt warred with the need to be alone. Now he was shutting Tamara out completely. *Snap.* The door was unlocked. But not open. He wasn't going to be able to undo that lie as easily.

At his desk he dropped onto the chair, hefted his feet on top of the desk and leaned back to stare at the ceiling, his hands clasped behind his head. His chest was pounding, his head starting to fill with haze.

'I am not having a panic attack.' He kept his elbows wide, refusing to let them fold in on his chest. He wasn't having an attack of any kind.

Except fear. Fear for Tamara and Sebastian. Fear that one day it would be her screaming in an emergency department as he left her to bring up their son alone. Fear that his little boy would spend years looking for him because he didn't understand what death meant.

The door opened and in walked Tamara, a mug in her hand and a wary smile on her face. 'Coffee.'

He wanted to say, 'Go away,' but the words refused to come.

She came around the desk to place the mug on the desk and stood there gazing down at him. 'Whatever you're thinking, Conor, it's too late. We are having a baby. The future may be an unknown on some levels but you're going to be a father and there's no changing that. Don't even contemplate becoming a remote parent. That would be far worse for Sebastian than the scenario I imagine is going on in your head right now.' Her kiss was soft on his cheek, her scent light. The bands around his chest loosened as she said, 'We're going to be fine.'

Then she left him to his thoughts, the door closing with a soft click behind her.

He went back to staring at the ceiling. 'You think?' How could Tamara be so positive? She'd been to hell and back, wore the scars from her own battles. Was strong because of them.

Could be a lesson here for you, boyo. Could be that Tamara is showing you a thing or two on how to grab life with both hands and enjoy it.

Could be he was wishing for the impossible. He did best by being alone.

Conor ran along the pavement circling the waterfront at Mission Bay, dodging around late-afternoon strollers enjoying the spring sunshine. His shoes slapped the concrete as he increased his pace, trying to outrun the torment in his head.

Tamara. She'd changed everything for him, given him hope, made him admit how much he wanted her and their baby. Yet he couldn't go through with it.

Stepping sideways onto the grass verge, he dodged around an elderly couple shuffling along arm in arm with smiles on their wrinkled faces. Beautiful. He wanted that. To do the whole lifetime-together thing with Tamara, to raise their child, or children, and be able to relax into old age and watch over everyone without getting too tied up in arguments and dilemmas. That's what he wanted. More than anything. But today reality had woken him up.

Increasing his pace until he was racing, not jogging at a sensible speed that'd last the distance, Conor sucked in abrupt breaths and ignored the occasional stabs of pain under his ribs. If he didn't leave the head stuff behind there'd be no peace. He ran and ran and ran until he could no longer put one foot in front of the other. Then he sank down onto a park bench and dropped his head into his hands, stared at the grass between his sports shoes.

The turmoil still pounded at him. Might as well have stayed at home. Or gone to the pub with Mac and sunk a few beers.

Might as well have visited Tamara and got this over and done with.

I don't want to hurt her.

I can't do what I'd planned on doing.

I can't live a lie.

I can't tip Tamara's world upside down again.

Conor's chest tightened. In a familiar, frightening way. He jerked up straight, his hands fisted, his legs tense.

Not now. Go away. Breathe, damn it, long and slow, deep. Breathe.

Damn, but he was a useless piece of work. He would not have a panic attack now. Not when he had to front up to Tamara. That'd be like asking for sympathy when he should be thrown down the street on his face. It was time to deal with these stupid attacks once and for all.

Pain stabbed him behind his sternum. Swift, hard, intense.

So you're going to make it hard for me.

Gritting his teeth, Conor waited for it to pass. If it would go. If this wasn't a genuine heart attack. He had been running like he was being chased by a hungry tiger.

Stab. He gasped around the second burst of pain. Breathed in long and slow, relaxed his lungs to push the air out again. Stood up and walked slowly forward six paces, walked back to the bench. Yeah, that worked. The tightness was easing.

Do it again. And again.

'I got a parcel today.' Tamara forced a smile, despite the unease ping-ponging back and forth between her and Conor. He'd turned up at her flat just as she'd been pretending to cook dinner. An inedible chop and spud were now in the bin. And Conor wasn't happy about something.

'About today—'

'From Ireland.' She reached across to her dining table and held up the express package.

Conor's eyes widened. 'That's Mam's handwriting.'

'She must've held a gun to the courier company's representative to get it here this fast.'

'Knowing Mam, she probably fronted up to the pilot on the next flight coming down this way and begged him to bring it. What's in there anyway?'

'Your first booties.' Her heart expanded. 'She kept them all this time.'

'I'm not that old,' Conor choked out.

'Judy has plenty more to send later. I think she must've been so excited she had to send these straight away.' Tamara tipped the booties out of the courier package and into her hand. 'Blue, not pink.' So soft, and cute. Adorable.

'Mam's not thinking straight,' Conor snapped.

Here it comes.

'Are you?' She pulled a chair out from the table and plonked her butt down. Her elbows hit the table top too hard. Her head was whirling with wanting to know what Conor's next move would be. Everything had happened so fast it had only been a matter of time before he stalled, and proved her right not to give in to the love growing in her heart for him.

'I'm trying to.' He sat opposite her, like they were strangers.

Maybe they were. Deep down where it counted. She started the ball rolling. 'Today brought home the enormity of what it would be like if the same thing happened to you as it did to your father.' Her voice hitched. 'And Sebastian.'

'In spades. Those deep, anguish-filled sobs got to me

in a way I've not felt before during my work in emergency departments.'

'I guess knowing we're having a baby makes it all the more real and worrisome. I understand that, Conor. I really do.' Tamara stood, went around to him and leaned in to kiss his mouth.

Conor's hands came between them, on her upper arms, holding her away. 'Tamara.'

Not Tam. *Thud, thud.* Her heart knew something was off. More than today's episode in ED. This tight, don't-be-hard-on-me feeling was familiar. She'd felt the apprehension before and knew it would lead to bad things. 'Tell me. Now.'

Conor's chest rose, and his gaze lifted to her eyes before his hands dropped away from her and he stood up. 'I'm sorry, Tamara, but I can't marry you.'

Why wasn't she in a heap on the floor? Her legs were like jelly and her heart had stopped. But standing she was, and in front of her was Conor, the man she'd believed in and come to accept wouldn't hurt her. All the moisture in her mouth dried up, and words were impossible as this rerun of her past unfolded before her. The man she'd foolishly fallen in love with when she'd known how dangerous that would be. Strange how the moment she learned he was leaving her she understood she really did love him.

'We'll still bring up Sebastian jointly. I'm not walking away from my son. Or my responsibilities.'

As the mother of your son, I'm one of your responsibilities.

No, she wasn't. Her life was her business, her problem. Not Conor's.

He looked pale and tense. But also determined. 'It might be easier if we have two homes in Sydney so that we're not tripping over each other all the time.'

Thought he'd enjoyed tripping over her, hauling her up against that divine body to kiss her whenever she got in the way. She sank back onto her chair. 'Why?'

'I've let you down. I'm sorry.' He stared out the window, his hands gripping his hips. What was he staring at? Seeing?

'Why?' she repeated over the clunking of her dreams breaking into tiny pieces. He'd never said he loved her, only proposed marriage to make it easier to raise their child together.

Conor leaned back against the windowsill. 'When I proposed I thought I could face anything with you at my side.'

'So what's changed?'

'I was fooling myself. I can't risk putting you through what my mother suffered.' Those dark eyes locked on her. 'I rushed into proposing before we'd talked through so many outstanding issues. I have been flying solo for so long, but for a few crazy days I let my guard down. I wanted to have the wonderful life you and our baby were offering.'

'You can. We can.'

'We can't.'

Anger began unfurling. He wasn't doing this to her. Not without a fight. 'You sure you're not using your medical history as an excuse?'

'I don't believe so.' Those lips were getting tighter by the word.

'So we're not getting married.' Her heart was curling in on itself, her stomach tightening defensively. Keep talking. 'We are having a baby, but we'll raise him in two homes, not one. We're moving to Sydney in the next couple of months.' Did he not see what she was saying? 'We, Conor. We, we, we.'

'I'll stay and apply for a permanent position in one of the hospitals in Auckland if you'd prefer.'

'Conor.' Her hands slapped her thighs. 'I don't want to change a thing.' She'd got it damned wrong. Again. Conor held her heart and he'd jumped on it. Unknowingly, sure, but it had happened.

She loved him through and through. Did that not count for anything? What if she told him how she felt? Just because she hadn't said those three little words it didn't mean they weren't real. She opened her mouth but the words would not come out. The last time she'd told a man she loved him he'd abused that love. And tonight wasn't going any better. How would saying it out loud help? Gulp. Swallow. She whispered, 'I do love you, you know.'

Conor jerked, like he'd been stabbed or something. 'Please, don't, Tamara.'

'Doesn't it mean anything to you?'

He stared at her, looking deep, as though absorbing her love. Then the shutters came down over those sad eyes, making them remote. 'All the more reason I let you go. Better to finish it now before we get too involved.'

Jamming her hands over her ears, she cut off that voice that usually had her in a rush of hormones. No rush tonight. More of an Irish bog.

Tamara asked in a wobbly voice, 'But you intend being there for Sebastian for ever? Will go wherever I decide to go for his sake?' A recipe for heartache on a daily basis. Seeing him, hearing his voice, conferring over what was right for Sebastian. She couldn't do it.

'I'm sure we'll be able to make it work without too many problems.'

That kind of suggested he didn't love her in any way. She'd gone and done it again. Fallen for the wrong man. Only this time she'd looked hard, thought it all through before giving her heart. And had still got it wrong. 'You think?'

Uncertainty worked into his gaze. 'I don't see you making it difficult for me. You're not a vindictive person.'

'You're making it sound so black and white, no grey at all.' Her voice was rising. Too bad. 'Think about it. What'll happen when you meet another woman who gets under your skin? Will she follow me around too?'

'I doubt that'll happen. I managed to stay uninvolved for nearly fourteen years.' He turned away, turned back, said softly, 'I'm setting you free so it's you who can meet someone else. A man without my health issues. A guy who can be a part of our child's life too. In case,' he ground out through clenched teeth. 'But I am not deserting my son. I will be a part of his life.'

'Just not mine.'

His hands slammed through his hair, setting it awry. 'Everything happened too fast. I should've thought about everything before my proposal.'

'You're not getting any argument from me on that score.' Tamara sat rigid, her hands gripped together between her knees. She would not beg Conor to rethink. He wouldn't listen. His mind was made up. As hers needed to be. She had to accept his withdrawal and get on with organising a future for her child.

Lifting her shoulders, she eyeballed this man who'd devastated her, and told him the biggest lie she'd ever uttered. 'Other couples manage two-family parenting so I'm sure we can. Now, if you haven't got anything else pressing to say, I'd like you to go.'

Her voice broke. Tears threatened. This time her grief would be private, not played out in front of even one person. Certainly not Conor. She could not show him how much he'd hurt her. He might use that against her. An hour ago she wouldn't have believed it possible; now she knew anything was conceivable. Her heart was a ball of pain and her stomach was churning. So not good for the baby.

'Tam.' He swallowed hard.

'It's Tamara to you.' Gulp. 'We were working just fine,' she snapped. 'Then you changed everything.'

'Maybe I did.' Sadness dripped off his words. 'We still have a lot of things to sort out and plan, but they can wait.'

Just go. Now. 'Get out of my home.'

Before I fall into a sobbing heap. Before I make an idiot of myself in front of you. Because once I do that you'll know you've done the right thing, that you definitely don't want to be hooked up to me for ever.

She sank further into the chair and covered her face with her hands. 'Go away.'

Conor's hand touched her head, gentle and warm, and shaking. 'I'll leave my key on the hall table.'

And she'd thought she'd been hurting before. A throbbing set up behind her eyes, under her ribs, in her gut. The key to her flat she'd been so happy to give him only yesterday because it showed she trusted him. He was giving it back.

The end.

CHAPTER TWELVE

NEXT MORNING TAMARA called in sick. 'I've got stomach cramps and a head full of cotton wool.'

'You're not going to Sydney for the weekend with Conor, are you?' Michael asked with a chuckle.

I wish. 'I could send you a selfie of me tucked up in bed, looking paler than a bottle of milk, but that'd be gross.'

Michael coughed. 'Didn't mean to sound uncaring. Maybe you should see your midwife if you're having stomach ache.'

Now, that would be the solution to all Conor's problems. Except she knew he'd be gutted if she miscarried. She'd be breaking down the midwife's door if there was any chance she was having a miscarriage. Her tummy wasn't too bad. Just showing its usual disgust at breakfast, probably made worse by anguish over Conor's desertion, and with lack of sleep thrown in. 'I think it's more what I ate for dinner than anything.'

'Keep vigilant and make an appointment if you think you're wrong. We'll see you on Monday.' Michael hung up.

All that was wrong with her was she'd been dumped by the man she really and truly wanted to spend the rest of her life with, and she couldn't face him today.

Her phone rang. 'Conor?' *Nope.* The screen showed Kelli.

'Are you all right, girlfriend?'

Tamara stifled the threatening tears. 'I'm wagging work.'

'Now I know there's something wrong. You don't take time off for anything.'

Calming breaths. 'I'm fine. A bit jaded. Think the pregnancy is taking its toll and what with everything else that's gone down these past days I'm exhausted. A day off is about the baby and looking out for him.'

'You're sure? I can come around at the end of shift.'

Sniff. 'Don't you dare. Come three o'clock you're on a week's leave, and I'm not going to be responsible for you missing that flight to Queenstown.'

'Okay, if you promise you're okay.'

'Promise.' Hopefully Kelli hadn't heard the crack in her voice. But in case she had, Tamara said goodbye and hung up. Now she'd lied to her best friend, but for all the right reasons. She wasn't subjecting Kelli to another round of her heartbreak.

Shuffling down the bed, Tamara pulled the sheet over her head and pretended to sleep.

Monday took for ever to arrive. Not that Tamara wanted to show up at work with the shadows highlighting her cheekbones and the shine gone from her eyes. Everyone would guess something was up between her and Conor. But working with patients to distract her was way better than hiding in her flat. There was only so much washing and dusting she could do and she'd done it all by midday Friday.

'Ambulance bringing in an elderly lady from Ponsonby. Found unconscious on her floor by a neighbour,' Michael told her. 'Can you take this one?'

'Cubicle three,' she acknowledged. 'How was your birthday?'

The morning dragged by, barely faster than the weekend had. Every turn she made, she fully expected to see Conor with a patient or reading patient notes or typing details into a patient's file or smiling at her. Every single time her gaze came up blank and her heart rolled over to belt her ribs. He was in Sydney and she missed him so much it was a permanent ache.

While she'd been in the shower yesterday, Conor had left a message on her answering machine that had quickly become her addiction. Hearing his voice was her only solace while at the same time it brought its own brand of agony. That Irish brogue stirred her deeply, tormented her and reduced her to tears every time she replayed the message. Not that she needed to hit replay.

'Hey, Tamara, heard you were off work on Friday. Hope you're not ill. I've made appointments to look at rental properties near the hospital next week. Will keep you posted. Oh, and you won't have a problem getting work at Sydney Hospital. Catch you.'

The actual words did nothing to comfort her. He sounded as though nothing was wrong between them. Unfortunately she couldn't stop listening to his voice.

Conor had left her. Sure, they'd get together over Sebastian, but that wasn't the same. That wouldn't satisfy her hormones, feed her desire, make her happy.

'Tamara, your patient's arrived in the ambulance bay.' A nurse nudged her.

Cripes. *Concentrate.* 'On my way.' Leaping up from the computer, her head spun and she had to grab the counter.

'Are you sure you should be back at work?'

'Didn't eat much over the weekend.' Stale bread was so not appetising. Neither was three-day-old salad. Hitting the supermarket was top of her to-do list after work today. The only thing on the list.

'Nearly three o'clock and home time,' a nurse eventually told her with sympathy in her tone.

'Great.' Home. Alone.

At home with a bag of heat-and-eat meals that didn't excite her taste buds but should keep baby happy, she made a cup of raspberry and pomegranate tea and sat with her feet up on the couch and the TV filling the empty space with background noise.

On her lap lay a courier parcel with Judy's handwriting scrawled over the address section. A bigger package than the last one, it had been sitting on her doorstep when she'd staggered up the path.

Should she even open it, considering she and Conor were no longer together? But Judy was still Sebastian's grandmother-in-waiting. As was her mum.

Putting the parcel aside, Tamara picked up her phone and hit 'Mum'. Listening to the endless ringing, she kept up a line of *Please, please, please.*

Finally, 'Hello?'

'Don't hang up. This is important.'

Click.

Write to her. Let her hold your letter, see your writing. Conor's advice wove around her, making her sit up straighter.

Did he have a point? Before she could overthink what she was doing, she scrawled two pages of news to her mother about her baby and moving to Sydney and sealed them in an envelope.

Then she picked up Judy's parcel and used her teeth to tear a hole big enough to push her finger through and rip it wide open. A teddy bear with one ear reattached with black thread and a leather patch stitched onto its front landed in her lap. Pressing it against her face, Tamara took a deep breath and smelled childhood and possibly Conor.

Soon the fake fur was saturated with tears, and still she clung to the bear. A letter had fallen out of the packet too.

Dear Tamara,

I hope you don't mind me sending you some of Conor's baby things, but I've waited so long for this day I can't hold back. Tell me to stop if you don't want any more parcels.

I know I'm being sentimental, but I love my son and know you'll be wonderful for him.

The page became a ball in her fist.

No pressure, Judy.

At least by now Conor's mother would know the score and was probably regretting sending the teddy. Lifting the bear, she stared at it, unable to toss it aside. It had been Conor's, would be Sebastian's.

Flattening the letter with her hand, she reread Judy's kind words, and through more tears felt her heart slow. Reaching behind her, she lifted her copy of the image of Sebastian taken during her scan. 'Sebastian, this is your teddy now. It used to be your daddy's. What do you think? Isn't he cute?'

Where was Conor? Swanning around Sydney like he hadn't gone and broken her heart? Chatting up his new colleagues, making himself popular?

Preparing for his son? And finding somewhere for her to live?

Damn it. She could find her own place. Didn't need his help. Certainly didn't want his input if he wasn't going to be a part of her life.

'Conor, I am missing you so much it's unbearable.'

Saturday afternoon Tamara listened to Conor's message one last time and hit delete.

For the hundredth time since he'd left, her heart broke all over again. He really had gone. Time to accept it and start planning the future.

If only Conor loved her then he wouldn't have left her. But he hadn't wanted to fall in love at all.

Just like she hadn't.

Ding-dong.

Her heart picked up its pace.

Conor? You've come back to spend the weekend with me, to make plans for our living arrangements and talk through your parting speech and maybe find a way out of this abyss.

Excitement rushed through her as she tugged the door open and swiped at the tears on her cheeks. She had another chance. He'd returned to try again.

'Oh, girlfriend, you look terrible.' Kelli was inside and hugging her before it completely hit home that Conor hadn't come back for her.

Her earlier tears had nothing on the flood now hosing out of her eyes, deep sobs racking her body.

Kelli held her until the storm abated. 'Conor?'

'H-he's g-gone,' Tamara hiccupped.

'That was the plan. To go sort out his new job and set up a place for you both to live.'

'He doesn't want to get married.' She started for the kitchen to put the kettle on. That'd give her something to do with her hands if nothing else.

'When did he tell you that?' Kelli demanded. 'I'm going to knock his block off for hurting you.'

'Thursday night last week.'

'That explains why you weren't at work last Friday. Why doesn't Conor want to get married? Changed his mind about loving you, has he?' There was an angry glint in Kelli's eyes that spoke of danger to Conor if he came anywhere close.

Water splashed over the front of her shirt when she turned the tap on too hard. 'He never said he loved me.'

'Has he got cold feet about becoming a father? Because leaving you doesn't change a thing about that. The baby is still going to arrive.'

'No, Conor would never shirk responsibilities. Anyway, he wants to be a part of Sebastian's life.' She nibbled her bottom lip.

'Then what's the problem?'

'He says he's protecting me from getting hurt if he has another heart attack.'

'What?' Kelli's question ricocheted off the walls.

Now she'd gone and spilled the beans. 'No one's meant to know but he had one fourteen years ago. He's terrified it'll happen again.'

Kelli sank onto a stool. 'Never saw that coming. But are you sure that's all? I mean, people have health problems all the time. Doesn't mean they don't get married and have families.'

'You don't think I didn't tell him that?' Tamara growled. 'I love him so much, it's crazy.' How was it so easy to admit that to Kelli when she'd struggled to tell the one person who mattered? The man who needed to hear it?

'There's not a person at work who doesn't know that. Same goes for Conor. He is totally smitten. I want to bang some sense into that skull of his.'

If only it was that easy. 'Tea?'

'You got anything stronger? Even if you're not drinking, with baby on board, I need something with more punch than tea. And it's wine o'clock somewhere.' Kelli grinned.

Opening the fridge, Tamara found a half-full bottle of wine Conor had left there. 'This do?'

'Yep.' Kelli got a glass from the cupboard and filled it to the brim. Bringing the stool to the bench, she perched on it and studied Tamara like she didn't know her.

'What?' Tamara demanded.

'You haven't told Conor how you feel, have you?'

'Yeah, I did. But it was like a last-minute confession, as though I was using my love to keep him here.' She looked away, ashamed at the censure in her friend's eyes. 'It wasn't easy to come right out with it, you know?'

'Sure it is. Don't let him get away, Tamara.'

Her head tipped up. 'That's what I've done, isn't it? Let him go without a fight. Wrecked everything for me and the baby.'

'Phone him, put your heart on the line. But don't beg, whatever you do.' Kelli's voice softened. 'He's nothing like Peter. Conor adores you and would never do a thing to hurt you.'

'He left for Sydney on last Friday without coming round to say goodbye, or—or anything.' Tamara hesitated. 'Sounds like I'm laying all the blame at Conor's feet, doesn't it?' Why hadn't she told him how hard it was to put her feelings into words? 'Is telling him I love him often enough going to make him shelve his fears? Or is there something else I can do?'

'There's only one way to find out. Put your heart on the line. You'll get an honest answer. He's not going to take advantage of you.'

'He talked me into writing to Mum.'

Kelli looked stunned. 'And you let him get away?'

Suddenly Tamara laughed. Where that had come from she had no idea, except that it felt as though a huge weight had lifted off her. 'I must be mad.' Or was that bonkers? Seemed she could fit right into Conor's family.

'I'd say so, but then you'd probably want to kill me.'

Another laugh. Slightly hysterical, but filled with relief. 'Just remember this advice you've been throwing at me. I can see a time coming when I'm going to give it all back.'

Kelli's smiled dipped. 'Not happening, girlfriend.'

We'll see. But not now, not today. Today—

'I'm going online to book a flight.'

'It had better be to Sydney.'

'Where else?' The laptop was already booting up.

'Want me to start packing some clothes for you?'

'What are my chances of a flight tonight?' Tamara stared at the screen, trying to hurry it up. Remembered to ask, 'How was your week in Queenstown?'

'Went mountain-climbing for three days. Awesome.' Kelli leaned over her shoulder. 'Looks like you're going to have to pay big money to go tonight.'

'Don't care. That seat's got my name on it.' Now she'd made up her mind to go to Conor, a shortage of cattle-class seats wasn't going to stop her. She clicked on the flight and filled in her details. Booked a seat. Business class no less.

Ding-dong.

'Get that for me, will you?' Tamara was entering her credit card number into the airline's booking page.

'Yes, Your Highness.' Kelli saluted. 'Do I get to drive you to the airport as well?'

'You don't think I can afford a taxi after paying top price for my ticket, do you?' There—number in…expiry date too. She pressed 'pay now' and watched the little circle go round and round and round. What was taking so long for the airline to grab the money?

'Tam?'

Her hand wobbled over the keyboard. She'd have sworn

she'd just heard an Irish lilt saying her name but that was impossible. Lack of sleep did strange things to her mind. Better get Kelli to check her booking to make sure she wasn't flying to Brazil next week.

'Tam.'

Don't do this, mind.

But she looked around anyway. And froze. 'Conor?'

Really? Truly? She closed her eyes. Opened them. *Yeah, really. Truly.*

'Conor,' she squealed, and leapt at him, wrapped her arms around that amazing body she loved and held on like she'd never let go again.

'Hey, Tam. You okay?'

The hesitancy in his voice changed her mind and forced her back, away from him. Just because he'd turned up here when he was supposed to be in another country, it didn't mean anything had been resolved.

'I'm fine,' she muttered.

Then she glanced at the table where the screen of her laptop showed her payment had been accepted. She was leaving for Sydney in four hours.

'No, I'm not. I'm all over the place.' Leaning across, she stabbed the 'continue' key on the screen and up came a ticket.

'What's that?' Conor asked, sounding confused. His eyes were fixed on the image.

'Take a closer look.'

He did. 'You were coming to see me.'

'Yes.'

'Why?'

Just do it.

'To tell you I love you. Tell you with all my heart this time. To ask you to reconsider about not being with me.' There. It hadn't hurt a bit. Conor hadn't started running for the hills. In fact, he looked stunned even as a smile began breaking out across his face. She said it again. 'I love you, Conor.' Dang, but that felt good. 'And I don't accept your reasons for calling off our marriage. I'm perfectly capable of coping with whatever happens. It might be messy but I'd pull through.'

'I know.'

'What do you know?'

'That you won't let me dictate what we're going to do in the future—about Sebastian and about us.' The smile widened, soft and warm and, oh, so sexy. 'I know you love me. You showed me countless times how much you cared about me. It was there in how you wanted to wait for me to go with you to that first scan. In how easily you chose Sebastian as the name for our son because it meant so much to me. I can't walk away from that.'

'What about your fears of another heart attack?'

The smile faded. 'They're always going to be there, and I'd worry about how Sebastian and you would manage even if I didn't live with you as my wife.'

'Conor Maguire, I would rather live with you than have to watch you from afar, no matter what the future brings us.' Tamara stepped up to him. 'Now, can we kiss and make up? It's been too long without you.'

Kissing Conor had always been her favourite pastime but this one surpassed them all.

'So you're back here and I'm flying out to Sydney shortly,' she teased.

His arms tightened around her. 'No, you're not, sweetheart. You're not going anywhere yet.'

'Oh, and what am I doing this afternoon, then?' Hang on. 'Kelli?' she called. 'Where are you?'

'She's gone. Just opened the door, saw me and kept on walking down the path with a great big grin on her dial.'

'That sounds like my friend.' She knew when she wasn't wanted.

'One in a million, I reckon.'

Tamara felt all her muscles melt as that Irish brogue washed over her. 'I've missed you.' She stretched up to kiss him but was stopped by two big hands on her upper arms.

'Wait.' Conor's expression turned serious.

Strange how that didn't worry her at all. He wouldn't have come back only to hand her another load of grief.

He took her hands in his. 'Tam, will you marry me?'

Damn, she was crying a lot today. 'Yes…' she choked. Then she shouted, 'Yes!'

His lips touched her cheek, oh, so gently. 'Can we set a date this time?'

'We could apply for a licence on Monday.'

'Could?'

'We're moving to Sydney, right? A new start for both of us. Why don't we wait and get married over there? It would give your family time to come out for the wedding too. If they want to.'

'Try keeping them away. You have no idea what you're letting yourself in for.'

'Yes, I think I do.' There was a teddy on the couch that explained a lot about how Conor's family loved each other. 'Can you kiss me again? There's been a drought this past week.'

Not only did Conor kiss her, he kissed her until she didn't know which way was up. And then he carried her down to her bedroom and followed through on the promise of that kiss.

EPILOGUE

THE SKY WAS bright blue and Tamara swore there was glitter in the air as she and Kelli walked along the promenade of Sydney's Darling Harbour towards to the restaurant she and Conor had chosen for their wedding. There were certainly bubbles every time she drew in a breath.

The bunch of daffodils she carried gave off a poignant spring smell and their colour was vibrant against the cream of her simple but stylish wedding dress that draped softly over her baby bump.

'Well, girlfriend, you're really marrying that gorgeous Irish hunk. You know every female back home in ED is so jealous?'

'Yes. And do I care?' She grinned at Kelli. 'This is the best day of my life.'

'I'd be worried if it wasn't,' Kelli retorted. 'I'm so happy for you.'

Along with a few special people, a small Irish crowd was attending her wedding and she couldn't be happier. All those bonkers sisters and their husbands and children had insisted they were coming out for the wedding with Judy and Dave. Tamara had fallen in love with each and every one of them the moment they'd walked through the arrivals doors at Sydney International Airport and drew her into their midst. When the end of Conor's stint in Australia came round she'd be pushing to move to Dublin.

At the entrance to the restaurant Tamara stopped and turned to hug her friend. 'Thank you for always being there for me. I'd never have got this far without you.'

'Shut up or my make-up will be wrecked when I start crying.'

'Too late.' Tamara made a discreet wipe at her own cheeks. 'Right, here we go.' And she stepped inside. Stopped, agape. Her heart thumped—hard. Her tummy squeezed. 'Conor...?'

From now on he was going to have to wear a suit twenty-four seven. The navy-blue fabric outlined his body to perfection, hugging his pecs, emphasising his wide chest and narrow hips. The crisp cream shirt highlighted his blue eyes and black hair.

'I'm going to faint.'

'No, you're not. Go get him, girlfriend.'

She took a step and he was there, reaching for her, taking her hand. 'You look more than beautiful,' he said.

Tamara locked eyes with her soon-to-be husband and sucked in a breath. Forget the suit. The look of pure love radiating out from those eyes just melted her. Completely. 'I love you.' Those words came so easily now that she couldn't believe how difficult uttering them had once been.

'And I you. Shall we do this?' Conor smiled and if her heart hadn't already melted it would've done so right then.

She nodded. 'Yes.'

Together they turned to walk up to the marriage celebrant. Conor's best man, Mac, stood on one side, dressed in nearly as amazing a suit. Glancing at Kelli, Tamara found her as awestruck as she'd been over Conor. Good. Maybe these two would finally get over what ailed them and learn to love each other.

'Tamara, darling, you look wonderful.'

She turned to face her mother, her poor overworked heart now beating against her ribs. 'Mum.'

Hard to believe that her mother had phoned out of the blue to ask when and where the wedding was happening. She didn't know it nearly hadn't happened, but the moment Tamara had told her it would be in Sydney in a month's time she'd been on her way to meet her grandson and take charge of planning the perfect wedding, with Tamara's aunt in tow. Tamara had happily given in. She was over not having her crazy mother in her life.

'I'm so glad you're here.'

'Oh, pish—as if I'd miss my own daughter's wedding.'

The words were cheap but the sentiment was strong. Typical Mum.

'You know that's not what I meant.'

Mum's smile said it all. 'Your father will be kicking up a storm, wherever he is.'

Conor was still holding her hand. 'Ready?'

'Absolutely.' They faced the celebrant, both smiling widely.

The woman cleared her throat and began. 'Tamara and Conor, today is very special for you both. Today is the beginning of a new life, and it's made more special with your families here to witness your vows.'

Tamara squeezed Conor's hand. Focused as she was on the celebrant's words, there was no not being aware of the man standing beside her. The man she loved more than she'd have believed possible. The father of her baby. The caring doctor. The good friend to Mac. Conor. Her about-to-be husband. The light in her heart.

'Tamara Washington, do you take this man to be your lawful wedded husband, and to love and cherish him for as long as you both shall live?'

'Oh, yes.'

'Conor Maguire, do you take this woman to be your lawful wedded wife, and to love and cherish her for as long as you both shall live?'

'Damn right I do.'

'Then you may place the ring on her finger.'

Conor dug into his pocket, apparently not willing to trust the ring to Mac. As he slid the wide gold band with an elegant emerald set perfectly in the centre onto her finger he whispered, 'Love you more than ever, Tam.'

The marriage celebrant had the last word. 'I declare you husband and wife. Conor, you may kiss the bride.'

Conor's kisses just kept getting better and better.

* * * * *

If you enjoyed this story, check out these other great reads from Sue MacKay

RESISTING HER ARMY DOC RIVAL
THE ARMY DOC'S BABY BOMBSHELL
DR WHITE'S BABY WISH
BREAKING ALL THEIR RULES

All available now!

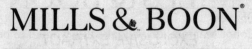

MILLS & BOON®

EXCLUSIVE EXTRACT

Lana Haole and the all-too tempting Dr Andrew
Tremblay agreed to a marriage of convenience… But
suddenly their convenient arrangement has become a
whole lot more!

Read on for a sneak preview of
CONVENIENT MARRIAGE, SURPRISE TWINS

Lana's request had caught him off guard, but he wasn't
displeased by it. Not at all. It was just that he couldn't.
He'd just never expected it from her. She was always so
careful, guarded, but the more time he was spending with
her, the more he realized a hot fiery passion burned beneath
the surface.

And that was something he wanted to explore, but he
had a sneaking suspicion that if he tasted this once, he
was going to want more and more. So, even though it
killed him, he left the room. Walked the beach, far away
from the wedding, to calm his senses, but it didn't work
because all he could think about was Lana's lips pressed
against his.

The feeling of her in his arms.

And her begging him to make love to her.

You can't.

Although he wanted to.

After what seemed like an eternity he returned to the
room. Hoping that everything had blown over, that she
might be already asleep even, but instead he saw her sitting
on the couch, a flute of champagne in her hand. She turned
to look at him when he shut the door and he could see the
tearstains on her cheeks.

Pain hit him hard.

He'd hurt her.

"Oh, I didn't expect you to come back," she said quietly and she wiped the tears from her face.

"I just needed a moment to myself."

"I see," she said quietly. Then she sighed. "Well, I think I'm going to turn in."

"Lana, I think we need to talk," he said.

"What is there to talk about?" She frowned. "You didn't want me and you have nothing to apologize about. I'm the one that wanted to step out of the boundaries we set. Not you."

"No, that's not it."

"What do you mean?" she asked, confused.

"I want you too, Lana. It's not for lack of desiring you. I want you. More than anything." And, though he knew that he shouldn't, he closed the distance between them and kissed her, fully expecting her to pull back from him the way that he had pulled from her, but she didn't. Instead she melted into his arms and he knew that he was a lost man.

Don't miss
CONVENIENT MARRIAGE, SURPRISE TWINS
by Amy Ruttan

Available July 2017
www.millsandboon.co.uk

Join Britain's BIGGEST Romance Book Club

- **EXCLUSIVE offers every month**
- **FREE delivery direct to your door**
- **NEVER MISS a title**
- **EARN Bonus Book points**

Call Customer Services

0844 844 1358*

or visit

millsandboon.co.uk/subscriptions

*This call will cost you 7 pence per minute plus your phone company's price per minute access charge.

CB3